TWO COWBOYS TO PROTECT HER

BLESSING, TEXAS

LACEY DAVIS

Can Two Texas Rangers Protect Her without Losing Their Hearts?

Rena Hall witnesses a horrible murder and the killer knows who she is. In the protective custody of two Texas Rangers, she soon realizes she wants more than just being protected. She wants her bodyguards to guard and protect her heart forever.

Harley Kerr and Clayton McCoy are Texas Rangers passing through Blessing when Rena comes running into the saloon to tell someone of a murder. But when they are asked to protect Rena, it's all they can do to keep their hands off her. And after one night of passion, they refuse to let her go.

But when she's kidnapped, will they rescue her before the killer ends her life?

Sign up for my New Book Alert and receive a complimentary book — Blindfold Me.

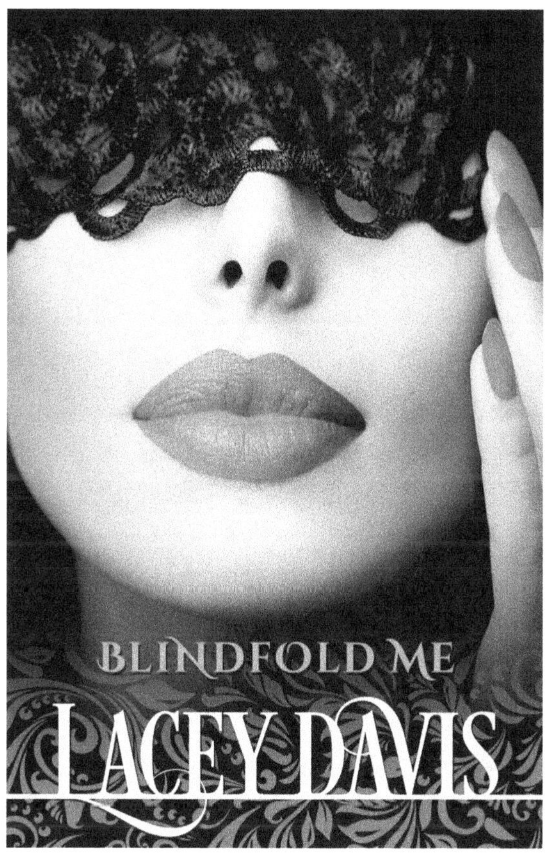

https://www.subscribepage.com/laceydavis_author

CHAPTER 1

It was late. Much too late for Rena to be out after dark, but the evening crowd at the restaurant where she worked lingered, and well, time got away from her. But everything was prepared for tomorrow morning's breakfast. Hopefully, the cook would be happy.

Now, nearly midnight, she walked on the edge of town to avoid going past the saloon. Saturday nights were the worst for the rowdy cowboys who came to celebrate. And Rena didn't want or need any trouble. Life was hard enough for a single woman without a family and a boring social life She didn't need to grab the attention of some drunken cowboy who just knew he could make her world complete once he took her to bed.

Rena wanted love, a family, children of her own and a man who adored her. Since her parents were dead and she didn't have a brother or sister nor aunts and uncles who lived nearby, she was alone.

Clouds covered the moon and leaves rustled sounding more like the rattling of snakes. A shiver traveled from the base of her spine to her head. No woman in her right mind would be out at this time of night.

What was she doing, taking such a risk?

A dog barked in the distance, and she glanced around in the darkness. Her home was only a couple blocks away, and she hurried to reach the door to her safe haven. Never again would she make the mistake of being out so late.

No matter what Jeremy the cook said about making certain everything was cleaned up before the next morning. Rena would not put herself at risk again unless she had a gun strapped to her waist or a man by her side.

If she had a man to take care of her, love her and give her the children she desired, she wouldn't be forced to work as a waitress any longer. She wanted love with a strong man who gazed at her like she was beautiful and made her heart flutter with desire. Someone who would marry her and show her what happened in the marriage bed. And eventually have children who would look up to him and call him Papa with pride.

A muffled cry of pain came from somewhere close and her heart almost leaped out of her chest. She stopped in the middle of the sidewalk and listened. There it was again.

Moving to the side of a building, she hid in tall bushes, praying no rattlesnakes slithered in the darkness. Slowly she moved forward until she came to the sight of a man strung up in a tree by his wrists, an older man whose large stomach hung over his belt.

A blood-curdling scream almost escaped her as she slapped her hands over her mouth. Her knees felt weak as fear overwhelmed her. The urge to run was swift, but she stood frozen in place staring at the half naked man who bleed from cuts on his flesh. His face was badly bruised and battered.

"Last chance," a large hulk of a man said. "Where is the map?"

"I've told you over and over again, I don't know," the man cried. "Don't you think I would give it to you, so you'd leave me alone?"

"You're lying. Who has it?" Another man with long dark hair stepped out of the shadows. She couldn't see his face.

The clouds cleared from over the moon and the

men's faces came into view. One had what looked like a birthmark on his face or a scar, she couldn't tell. The second man had a mustache and beard. They both wore well-worn shirts with leather chaps covering their thick thighs.

The bearded man took a knife and sliced a piece of flesh off the hanging man's side. He screamed and Rena wondered why no one heard his anguished filled cries. The houses were down the road, but still they were close enough residents should have heard him. She didn't know the victim's name, but he had come into the restaurant a couple times.

"I want the map. I'm not leaving without it. "

"Leon has it," he cried in anguish. "Now, please, let me down."

The two men looked at each other and laughed. "Leon? Leon Roberts?"

"Yes," he said. "My papa got in a bind and sold it to the man. There is no treasure. My father searched for it for years. It's gone."

The man with the dark spot on his face held his knife up under the man's chin. "You're wrong. My great-grandfather stole the silver from Jean Lafitte and hid it along the Guadalupe River. Your great-grandfather is the thief who took the map showing the location of the treasure. I'm going to find Leon, kill him, and take the map."

The man hanging by his wrists seemed defeated. Blood dripped from the cuts he'd suffered. The men had tortured him to get their answers.

"I should scalp you like the Indians do," the man hissed. "Your family is the reason mine is not rich."

The man opened his glazed eyes like he was seeing earth for the last time. He stared at him with repulsion, then he spit on him. "Fuck you."

A cry of rage came from the outlaw, and he stabbed the man, driving the knife deep.

A squeal escaped from Rena and the two men twirled around and glared at the bushes where she hid. Her heart plummeted to her feet.

What the hell had she just done? But the murder was brutal, and even now, terror seized her. She had just witnessed the death of a stranger.

"Who's there?"

They started walking toward her, and she lifted her skirts and ran like her life depended on it, because it did.

No longer caring about snakes, she ran knowing if they caught her, she was dead.

Life at twenty-eight was a lot different than his younger years, but still Harley Kerr's past rode him hard. Sitting at a table with his partner in the Blessing saloon, he stared at the telegram from his father.

Rage filled him like a Texas river flash flood. How had the man found him and what the hell made him contact him after almost eight years? Hell would freeze over before he forgave his old man.

"What does he want?" his friend and partner in the Texas Rangers asked.

"For me to come to work for him. He's offering me ten thousand dollars to work at the mercantile with him," Harley said with a sigh. "Hell, when I was a kid, he barely gave me a nickel a day to work for him."

Clayton shook his head, his long dark hair brushing his shoulders. "What are you going to do?"

That was the million-dollar question. He was tired of being a Texas Ranger. Of chasing after bad guys and always being on the road. No, he wasn't old, but he'd been doing this for almost ten years, and it was time to settle down. Time to get off the road.

Being a ranger was not the occupation for a husband and father. And he wanted to be both. Surely, he could do better than his old man had. Hell, anyone could be a better father than his. All that was required was to keep your fists to yourself.

"Don't know yet," he said, stuffing the telegram in his pocket. "He's trying to worm his way back into my life. Why in the world would I put myself in a position for him to abuse me again? Why would I help that bastard?"

"There is the store. It's your inheritance," Clayton said.

Maybe so, but not really what he wanted in life.

"If the old man was dying, I might consider it, but he's just putting out the offer of ten thousand dollars as bait to draw me back to the fold."

For a moment, he considered his brothers and sisters and wondered if they had fared any better than he had with their papa.

A fight broke out in the corner by the card tables.

Men were screaming to stop before they went for the sheriff.

All the anger rose inside him. Right now, it was what Harley needed. He got up from his chair and felt his face tightened as his hands curled into fists.

"Harley," Clayton warned.

Strolling over to the fight, he yelled at the two men, "Texas Ranger. Don't give me the pleasure of arresting you two. Or if you do, please resist. My fists need something to punch."

The men halted and glanced at him, breathing hard.

"I don't see no badge," the younger man said.

Harley's insides tensed as he walked up to the young kid.

"You don't have to see my badge." He grabbed him by the collar and lifted the man. "My partner is behind me, and after the day I've had, I'd love nothing better than to use you for a punching bag. You up for the challenge?"

The man's eyes widened. "No."

"I didn't think so," he said, wishing he could have gotten a few punches in.

Knowing he was out of line, but still trembling with the need to hit something, he released the man. "Now, I'm going over there to finish enjoying my drink. Don't make me get up again or I'll haul your ass down to the city jail in pieces."

"Yes, sir," both men said.

Harley returned to his table and sank down across from Clayton.

"Sons of bitches," he said softly.

In a few minutes, the waitress brought a second shot of whiskey. "From the bartender. He said thank you."

People returned to drinking or playing cards.

"No problem," he said, lifting the glass in the man's direction.

This was why he became a law officer, protecting and helping people unlike anyone had helped or defended him and his mother. No one was there for them, so he was determined to be there for others.

The first nine years had been good and he'd gotten much of his frustration out by catching criminals, but now he was ready for a different kind of life. And as much as he didn't want to take his father's offer, it was intriguing.

"That telegram has really riled you up," Clayton said.

"I'm torn. My father is the devil, and I would never want to return to work for him, but yet, I'm tired of riding the range, always being on the road. I'm ready to settle down. Find a woman, have a couple of kids. Hopefully, be a better father than my own dear old papa."

Clayton glanced around the saloon. "For years, we've talked of trying to find a woman who would agree to be our wife, who would agree to our lifestyle. But it's hard to find someone when you're always traveling."

The tinny piano began to play again, and Harley glanced around to see if the two men fighting had left. They were nowhere to be seen.

"You know, most Texas Rangers either quit or are killed. It's not a job for a family man. Or even being able to find a woman you could love forever. If we weren't working, we'd be searching for a woman to share between us."

"Amen," Clayton said. "I'm agreeable to the idea of finding a woman to share for life, but only if we buy a ranch. I'm not willing to live in town and have your father interfering in our lives all the time. That's not for me."

This was what Harley was afraid of. If he took the money and the position his father offered, the man would think he owned him again. The money was tempting, but he didn't know what to do. No matter how much he hated his father, the little boy inside him hoped he had changed. Hoped that he would accept him.

Suddenly a scream cut the air and he glanced over to see a woman being forcibly dragged from the saloon.

After the abuse his mother went through, this was what angered him the most. Oh hell, no. A man did not have the right or the privilege to harm a woman.

Jumping up from his chair, he knocked it over and all but ran to the woman's side.

"What the hell is going on here?"

"None of your business," the man with a long red scar on his face said, his eyes were dark and evil.

"She's my wife and she disobeyed," he said.

"No, I'm not, please help me. He's going to kill me," she cried. "There's been a murder."

"Shut the fuck up," the man said as he back handed her across the face.

The woman screamed and that was Harley's final rational thought. All the turmoil inside him broke loose as his fists curled and connected with the man's face.

He grabbed the man's shirt, and the jerk released the woman to hit Harley, but he ducked.

"You son of a bitch," Harley growled. "No one has the right to hit a woman."

The woman stood on the fringes staring at them.

"Don't interfere," the big, rugged man said.

Harley punched him in the face again. "I'm a Texas Ranger and I can interfere any damn time I want. Now get your ass out of here before I haul you off to jail."

The man staggered back, nose broken. He glanced at the woman. "Keep your mouth shut, do you understand me? I'll be looking for you."

"He killed a man," she cried.

The man was shaking and Harley wondered what that was about. The man suddenly ran out of the saloon.

When Harley turned to look at the woman, Clayton was holding her in his arms while she cried. He stared at her blonde hair and emerald eyes covered with long dark lashes. Beautiful.

Gazing at her, it was like Harley was kicked in the chest. Like Cupid pulled back his bow and the arrow pierced his heart. Clayton had his arms wrapped around her and staring at him as if saying *don't you wish you were holding her?*

His cock sprang to attention while his heart did a little pitter-patter.

"It's all right."

"No," she said, shaking her head. "I must speak to the sheriff. They killed a man. I saw it and that's why he's after me."

Once again the saloon had gone quiet. Had he just let a murderer go? She had said he had killed a man, but was it true?

"We'll escort you down to the sheriff's office," Clayton told her. "No one is going to harm you."

"The sheriff is in bed," one of the men standing around said.

"If there is a murder, he needs to know," Harley said.

"Someone fetch him from his bed. We'll meet him down at the jail."

"Thought you were Texas Rangers?" another man said.

The woman glanced at him. "You're Texas Rangers?"

"Yes," he said.

"Thank God. There is a man strung up in a tree on the edge of town. I saw them murder him."

She would need protection and Harley knew they were just the men to take care of the gorgeous woman. He glanced at Clayton and knew he was thinking the same thing.

"Don't worry, we'll keep you safe," he said. "Stay with Clayton while I find the body."

If the woman was smart, she would obey him and stay with Clayton. If not, he'd be tempted to turn her over his knee and give her a spanking. But never hard enough to hurt her. Never would he beat a woman. Never.

CHAPTER 3

"Shh, we're going to keep you safe," Clayton said to the woman in his arms, repeating what Harley had just said as they all stood in the saloon.

"I live on the south end of town and he's hanging in the trees not far from my home. That man stabbed him."

Clayton kept his arms around her, feeling her body shake. Harley sent him a jealous look and then he turned and walked out the door.

When she had first screamed and he saw that big burly man pulling her to the door, it was then that the two of them raced toward her.

Anger fueled his partner and drove him to oftentimes be more aggressive than Clayton cared for, but the man had the devil burning up inside him. A rage at the way his father had beaten him and his mother until Harley left.

Now, Clayton tried to keep his partner from going too far when he got in a fight. But when he'd seen this beautiful woman struggling against the man, even Clayton felt his insides turn to mush.

It was like the heavens opened and he could hear angels singing and knew that whoever she was, he had to get to her and protect her. And, damn, if he got the chance, have her too.

The woman was stunning and when he saw her crying, his first thought was to comfort her. When he wrapped his arms around her, she had laid her head on his chest and sobbed. As she trembled in his arms, he'd done his best to make her feel protected, her heart thudding against his chest, his dick hard and crying out *yes*.

"Come on," Clayton said, "let me take you to the sheriff's office."

He took her by the elbow and led her from the saloon, away from the noise and cowboys standing around gawking at the fight.

"I'm Clayton McCoy," he said. "Texas Ranger."

"Rena Hall," she said softly as they walked down the steps and into the night air that was cleansing from the smoke and chaos inside.

Glancing around, he tried to make certain no one

was hanging around to ambush them as they came out the door. The poor woman didn't need another fight over her tonight. He could see her wariness as they strolled down the darkened street, his hand near his six-shooter.

"What are you doing out so late at night by yourself?"

Tears welled in her eyes. "I'm a waitress cook at the local restaurant here. It was late when we finished, and I walked the long way home to avoid the saloon. Guess I would have been safer going this direction."

He pulled her closer as they walked down the street, his eyes searching the darkness. The man who was after her was very intent on her leaving with him.

"Was that man the one who killed your brother?"

She shook her head. "He's not my brother. I don't know who he is, but he lived here in town. He often came into the restaurant."

"So, you just walked up on them killing him?"

A shiver went through her. "Yes. I hid in the bushes when I heard him cry out. They were trying to get him to give them a map. And after he admitted that he didn't have it and told him that Leon Roberts had what he wanted, they killed him."

When they arrived at the sheriff's office, it was vacant and he led her inside. Gazing around, he saw the lantern and quickly struck a match and lit the wick.

In the glow of the light, he could see she was just as beautiful as he first thought. There was an innocence about her that he found intriguing. That he wanted to conquer.

Her hands were still shaking. "How did you get away?"

"When they stabbed him, I made a noise and then they came after me. I ran as fast as I could to reach the saloon. It was the only place still open. I don't know what happened to the second man, but he didn't follow me."

Clayton suddenly had a feeling they were not going to find a body hanging on the outskirts of town. The one who stayed behind was getting rid of the body in order to make Rena's story look doubtful.

Without a body, they couldn't make an arrest and the only evidence they had was her word.

Glancing at her, it was all he could do not to pull her in his arms again, but he didn't want to scare her away.

"Are you all right?" he asked her. "Why don't you sit down until the sheriff gets here."

"They're not going to find a body, are they?"

"Probably not," he said, not wanting to lie to her. "While he was chasing you, the other man would have disposed of it."

"I wish I could remember his name," she said, sinking

down into a chair. "He came into the restaurant several times and ate alone."

A quick glance at her hand revealed there were no wedding rings. But she might have other family members.

"Do you live alone?"

"Yes," she said. "My papa died three years ago and here I am. A single woman working to support myself, living alone, and now I have a crazed killer after me."

Sadness filled her eyes and he realized she didn't like being alone.

"A beautiful woman like yourself doesn't have some man courting you?"

"No," she said. "I guess I'm too poor for the young men in town to be interested in me."

They were all fools then. Those emerald eyes that flashed her every emotion and the way her lips pulled into a pout made him want to slant his lips over hers and kiss away every problem she had. Or better yet, to feel those lips wrapped around his cock.

What the hell was wrong with the single men in this town? Were they blind?

But Clayton was a tainted man, not one who deserved a woman like her. Still, that didn't stop his body from reacting to her sweet smile, and how just glancing at her, he imagined her full breasts filling his hands and her legs wrapping around him as he plunged into her wet and willing pussy.

She may be poor, but she didn't have the stain of a mother who had been a whore, and he was the result of one of her clients. A father he would never know.

Just then the door to the sheriff's office opened and Harley strolled in along with the sheriff.

"No body was found."

Exactly what Clayton feared would happen. Now it was their word against Rena's.

"I know what I saw, and when that man plunged the knife in that man's body, it killed him. Blood was pooling on the ground. Maybe it's time I went home if none of you are going to believe me."

Rena stood and shook her blonde curls, her back straight as she marched to the door. The woman had a strong spirit and that made Clayton admire her even more.

Harley stepped in front of her. "Wait, we didn't say we didn't believe you. We just said there was no body there."

Clayton stood within inches of her, and his partner's breathing was fast and clipped. A whiff of her perfume drifted to Clayton's nose and he wanted to groan.

"Harley Kerr, by the way," he said, holding out his hand and taking her small one in his.

"Rena Hall," she said.

The sheriff stepped close to Rena. "Sit down and tell us everything you saw and what happened. I didn't get out of a nice bed not to hear your side. Tell me everything."

She licked her lips nervously as if touching Harley made her nervous. Finally, she sat. For the next ten minutes, she told them how she left the restaurant and how she came upon two men torturing this poor soul.

As Clayton listened, he wanted to comfort her and tell her everything was going to be all right. That they would protect her and keep her safe. That all her troubles were now his. And yet, there were no guarantees.

When she told them all she saw, the sheriff questioned about what the men looked like.

"We saw the one who followed her to the saloon," Harley said. "He had a scar running down his cheek."

The sheriff reached back and pulled out a wanted poster. "Was this the man?"

"Yes," she said, excited.

"Yes," Harley confirmed.

The sheriff shook his head. "That's Jack Bell of the Red Jack Gang. There are only two of them. Shotgun Tray Lander is his partner, and those two men are mean."

"Do you think they know where I live?"

The man didn't answer. "Hard to know, but it wouldn't be too difficult to find you."

"I live alone," she said. "I don't even own a gun."

This was the opportunity Clayton was looking for. Not that they would ever take advantage of her, but to spend more time with the lady was what he was praying for.

"We'll stay with you," Harley said.

It was all Clayton could do not to grin. They knew each other so well.

"Yes, we'll walk you home and then we're not going to leave you, because those men will be back to kill you."

She closed her eyes for a moment. "I appreciate you offering to stay with me, but I'm a single woman living alone. Two men staying at my house would upset my neighbors and ruin my reputation."

Clayton stepped up to her. "Honey, do you want to live or save your reputation?"

A heavy sigh came from her and then she shook her head. "You can't stay with me all the time. I'm sure you're here on a case."

"We are," Harley said. "This case, now. Actually, we were going to come see the sheriff in the morning and then move onto the next town. But now we're going to catch this murderer."

Glancing between them, she bit her lip nervously. "I can trust you?"

They grinned at each other. "We only accept willing women," Clayton replied.

"Yes," Harley said. "Our job is to protect and keep you alive."

When she licked her lips, it was all Clayton could do not to grab her and experience that full, soft mouth and hear her whimper and cry out his name.

"All right," she said. "Until you catch them, you can stay."

CHAPTER 4

As they walked the darkened streets on their way to her home, she couldn't help but think it felt like she was sneaking home. Only this time, she had two very handsome lawmen with her, who made her breath shallow and her heart thump wildly when they touched her. The most handsome men she had ever met.

Harley's serious dark eyes and head full of dark hair, his muscled arms and broad chest made her feel protected as she walked between them.

And Clayton, the man who held her and let her cry on his chest. His big, burly arms encompassed her, and she'd never felt safer. With his cropped, sandy-brown hair and blue eyes, she wanted to reach up and pull his mouth down to hers. To lose herself in that sky-blue gaze and those luscious full lips.

Never had she experienced feeling this way about not one, but two, men and now they were going to stay at her home to protect her. She'd never felt more nervous than she did now. Her home was small. Two bedrooms, a kitchen, and small living area.

"Where did the murder happen?" Harley asked.

Fear rippled through her as they stopped. "It was here. There should be blood on the ground."

Clayton laid a hand on her back as if to reassure her. "We'll come back and check it out in the morning. Right now, let's get you home."

They kept walking toward her home. Rena was so bone tired, she could barely keep up. She couldn't wait to collapse.

Suddenly, Harley's hand held her up and they all stopped and listened. "Where is your house?"

"Last house on this block," she whispered. Suddenly, a man ran out the back door of her home.

"Someone's been inside," she cried. "Stop him."

The two men raced after him, but he disappeared into the woods where he had a horse waiting. She watched as he jumped on and rode off. What had he been searching for?

Harley and Clayton came hurrying back to her. "Was it the same guy?"

"I don't know. But why would anyone else be breaking into my home?"

As far as she knew, she had no enemies. While she had lived in Blessing most of her life, her family was poor and they didn't have much. Now that she was alone, she realized she didn't know as many people as she thought. No one seemed to care about an unmarried woman living on the edge of town.

She opened the door, there was no sense sitting out here wondering what he'd been doing in her home.

"No, let us go in and check everything out. You wait right here," Harley said.

The deep timbre of his voice sent chills trickling down her spine.

"Stand back in case we come running out," Clayton told her, taking her by the shoulders and placing her where he wanted her. The touch of his hands made her breathing increase.

What was it about their touch?

What was it about these men? Oh, how she prayed neither one was married, because her imagination was swarming with ideas of what it would feel like to be their woman. To feel their hands on her. To touch her intimately.

But she could only have one. Which one would she choose? Harley with his serious dark eyes and protective fists or Clayton—slow, sweet, and caring.

"Be careful," she warned not wanting anything to happen to either one of them. She didn't know which one she would pick, but they were both what she wanted.

They slipped inside the door, and she saw Clayton light a lantern. From the glow, she could see them moving through the house. Since it was small, it didn't take long.

"Come on in," Harley told her.

Standing outside, she'd felt nervous and she all but ran into the house.

"Can you tell if anything is missing?"

Walking through, she lit another lantern and gazed about. When she went into her bedroom, she noticed her father's prized golden pocket watch was gone. She always laid it on the table next to her bed so she knew the time.

"My papa's watch is missing," she said with a sigh. Sure, it wasn't worth much, but it was all she had of the man who raised her. Tears welled in her eyes and she bowed her head. This day had been a nightmare.

She felt hands on her shoulder and Harley turned her into his arms and held her while she cried. Both of these men had comforted her, and she felt a sense of protection overwhelm her. His lips touched her forehead.

The mattress of her bed, bumped against the back of her legs and she realized they were in her bedroom, near her bed.

"Thanks," she said. "It was all I had left of his things."

"We'll do our best to get it back," he promised her as he leaned back and gazed at her.

Warmth spread through her, and she believed him. Why she felt comfortable with these two strangers, she didn't know, but she did. And they were standing in her bedroom. A very personal space.

Pulling out of his arms, she turned to leave, and Clayton stood in the doorway gazing about the room.

"Is this where you sleep?"

"Yes," she said breathless that they were in her bedroom. Thank goodness, she'd cleaned the house before she left yesterday morning. "There is another bedroom that the two of you can share."

They smiled, and first Clayton and then Harley backed out of the doorway, making her feel more comfortable. While she had been told about the marriage bed, she also knew that sometimes men took advantage of a woman, and she was in a very vulnerable position.

"Are you hungry?" she asked, thinking the least she could do was cook for them.

"Yes," Harley said.

"Actually starving," Clayton replied. "We didn't get into Blessing until after the restaurant had closed, so anything would be wonderful."

She grinned. One thing she could do was cook. Since she had worked at the restaurant these last three years, she'd learned to cook.

"I'll fry up some eggs," she said. "First, let me show you where you'll be sleeping."

Even as she said the words, she felt awkward. Two strange men sleeping in her home, which had not seen another person since her father died.

When she moved past them, her skirts brushed against both men's legs sending her heart fluttering with excitement.

Harley had kissed her forehead. While she didn't think that was a huge thing, it had comforted her and made her feel like he was trying to ease her fear. No one had been around to make her feel better in years. It felt good that another person wanted to share her burdens.

After she had shown them their room, she went into the kitchen and they followed her and sat at the table.

"How long have you lived here," Harley asked her.

"All my life," she said. "My mother died in childbirth

when I was ten and my father raised me. Then he passed away three years ago, and I've been alone since then."

"No other brothers or sisters?" Clayton asked.

"No, when Momma died, the baby did as well. So it was just me and Papa," she said. "Now, it's just me."

Harley suddenly stood, his chair scrapping across the wooden floor. "You're in danger. It's not safe for you to live here alone."

"And just where do you think I would go? I've been all right the last three years," she said.

He put his finger under her chin and lifted her face to meet his eyes. "But you're no longer safe. This man is looking to find and kill you."

There was that small complication, but what did he expect her to do? As it was, she lived on so little. Her salary went to buy groceries and a few minor things, but she had nothing. And if she couldn't work, she'd have even less.

Clayton was at her side. "You need to marry."

Quickly, she finished the eggs. Turning, she grabbed the plates. The two men had surrounded her, and she gazed up at them, her brows lifting. "I know, but I haven't met a man that I would have. I'm not taking just any man. My man has to be a man our children would look up to."

She would take either one of these two men if they were as honest and trustworthy as she believed.

"Your eggs are getting cold," she said, handing them a plate.

They took the plates from her and sat at the table. Quickly, they ate the bacon and eggs and toast.

Leaning back, Clayton grinned at her. "Thank you. I feel much better now that I've eaten."

"Good," she said. "After how you helped me, it's the least I can do."

She picked up the dishes from the table and stacked them in the sink. The water pump was outside, and while she'd never been afraid before, now she felt nervous about going out there at night.

Tonight, she just wanted to get to bed to rest and recuperate from the long, stressful day.

"I think I'll leave the dishes until in the morning," she said.

Feeling anxious, she glanced at the two men who were staring at her. "I'm going to try to get some sleep now. I have to work in the morning."

"No, you can't go in," Harley said. "It's too dangerous."

"I have no choice. It's how I make my living," she said. There was no way she could miss work without being fired.

The two stared at each other and she could tell they were communicating without saying a word.

"Clayton will go in to work with you tomorrow. He'll hang around until you can leave."

The thought of the big, burly man at her side all day long was nerve-racking and yet it was also comforting. Nervous because he made her feel things she'd never experienced before and comforting because with him there, she would be safe.

"Good-night, gentleman," she said and knew they watched her as she left. Would they keep their word tonight and not try to impose themselves on her? And what if they did? Right now, every time she looked at them, her heart sped up and her lungs squeezed making it difficult to breathe.

An innocent, she didn't know if these feelings were normal or if she was a wanton woman.

CHAPTER 5

After Rena went to bed, Harley and Clayton retired to the other bedroom. Her house wasn't large and Harley was certain they would be able to hear if anyone tried to break in. As they entered the room, his partner shook his head.

"Damn, I just want to go in there and fuck her," Clayton said. "She needs us and we need her."

Setting the lantern down, Harley stared at the small room that had a dresser and a bed that would barely hold the two of them. The woman had so little.

Harley turned and glanced at his best friend, a man he considered his brother, who he would share everything he had with. Including women. They had shared whores, but this was different. This woman was as innocent as pure snow. And it would give him nothing but pleasure to introduce her to the ways between a man and a woman.

To claim her and make her theirs.

"She's naive and very vulnerable."

"Yeah, I know and right now my cock is hard as a rock. We would be her first."

"No, this kind of woman deserves a ring on her finger."

Women like Rena were to be adored, protected, and loved. All his life, he'd promised himself that his wife would be like a queen, and in the bedroom, he would be her king. Never would he treat a woman like his father had his mother.

Oh no, his wife would be respected and admired and loved beyond measure.

"But you haven't made up your mind about what you want to do. I'm not going to Dallas to work for your father."

The old man had accomplished exactly what he set out to do. He'd laid out the bait to draw Harley home, and though he was resisting the temptation, the money would be so easy. The man had also driven a wedge between him and Clayton. Something that had never happened.

"Give me some time. Give Rena some time. She doesn't realize the danger she's in and sooner or later this is all going to come to a head."

Clayton nodded. "I would never push myself on her, but if she would have the son of a whore, I would ask her to marry me. I'm not the best she could do. But at least, we could protect her permanently. Not just right now, but forever. I'm staying with her tomorrow."

As much as Harley told his best friend that nobody cared about his heritage, the man refused to believe he was worthy because his mother had worked in a brothel and he didn't know who his father was. His friend had a heart of gold and would help anyone. Someone who accepted everyone and tried to give back.

While Harley had a heart of stone, Clayton was the softie who often kept him from being too harsh. He took the edge off Harley and that was a good thing.

"Man, she is one fine woman," Clayton said. "The moment I laid eyes on her, I was smitten. Nice rounded curves, long legs to grip a man and such a sweet little ass."

"Yes, and she seems stubborn," Harley said, thinking he could detect a bit of fire inside Rena. A fire he would love to stroke into a blaze. A blaze he controlled.

"It's decision time. This woman is perfect, and if she would have us, I'd marry her in a heartbeat," Clayton said. "You need to make up your mind about wanting a ranch or going to work for your papa."

Since the moment he received the telegram, it had been a constant pressure that ate at him. What should he do?

The two men shucked their clothes and stretched out on the bed. A cool breeze blew in from the window.

"We could be in there right now fucking her," Clayton said.

"Not without a ring," Harley reminded his friend.

"Agree, but if she would take both of us, I think she's our woman."

The woman was so innocent, he wondered if she had even heard of a marriage with more than one husband. The thought of bending her over his knee and rubbing her smooth white cheeks before he popped her on the ass had his dick throbbing.

"This is going to be a long night," Clayton replied. "It's hard to sleep when there is such a gorgeous woman right down the hall that needs us."

Harley laughed. "I think the need is the other way around. You need a woman."

Clayton sighed. "I do," he said. "And she's the one I want. We're going to be here for a few days, so let's just see how things go. But I can't wait to strip her naked and have her spread between us."

The thought of Harley shoving his cock deep inside her was enough to make him groan. No matter how they felt about her, they would both respect her wishes and not let their desire overcome them.

"I agree. We need to find the Red Jack Gang and locate the body of the murdered man. Also find her papa's pocket watch."

Lying there looking up the ceiling, he thought about the case, trying to ease the ache between his legs.

"Do you believe there is a map showing where silver is buried?"

"It's been rumored for years, but who knows if it's true or not. But to kill a man who tells you he doesn't have the map, that's cold," Clayton said in the darkness.

The breeze picked up from the open window and the curtains billowed out.

"We need to ask around town if anyone else has heard about this mysterious map."

"Yeah, the next few days are going to be busy. I'm jealous that you're going to get to stay with Rena tomorrow."

Clayton laughed. "We'll take turns. The next day you can stay with her. But the first time you kiss her, I'm going to be jealous."

"Already have. I kissed her on the forehead earlier tonight."

"Son of a bitch. I've wanted to kiss her on the lips all night long," Clayton said. "But I held back."

Harley laughed. "That's next. Oh, yes, that's next, and I'm going to shove my tongue right down her throat."

"Well, that gives me something to work toward tomorrow," Clayton said. "This sweet little woman is going to be ours."

CHAPTER 6

*R*ena slept very little that night, tossing and turning. Every time her eyes closed, she would see the man hanging from the tree and once again witness his killing. Then Harley and Clayton would enter her dream and show her the pleasure between a man and woman.

A moan would awaken her to the feel of her fingers between her legs, pleasuring herself.

She didn't know why she was thinking about them, but it was such a pleasant feeling after experiencing the nightmare that she didn't care.

Either man would be perfect for her and yet she knew they would never be interested in a woman like her.

Early the next morning, she dressed for work. In the

dawning light when she walked out the door, she saw a man off in the distance watching her. He smiled and fear seized her as she hurried back into the house, her heart pumping wildly.

After she closed the door, she leaned against it. What was she going to do? If she missed work, she would be fired, but the thought of that man catching her was terrifying.

That was the man from the night before. Not the one who chased her, but the one who hid the body.

Harley and Clayton must still be asleep and she needed to get to work.

Knocking on their door, she heard a groan. Slowly she opened the door and stood there in shock. Both men were naked as the day they were born. Their cocks lay hard against their bellies, smooth and long and so irresistible.

For a moment, she just stared at the two of them. Their hard muscled chests, their thick burly arms and the manly smell that filled this room. Not a bad odor, but one that tantalized her. One that made her want to cuddle between them.

Taking a step back, she closed the door. It would not be proper for them to catch her staring at their naked bodies in awe. She'd never seen the male physique and she had the most incredible urge to run her fingers down their chest until she reached below their waist and take their cocks in her hands.

Not something a young, single woman should be thinking about.

Once again, she knocked. This time a little louder. "Clayton, it's time for me to leave for work."

She heard him rustling around. Thank God she'd stepped out the room before he awakened. "Give me a minute," he called out.

Walking away from the door, she peeked out the hall window to see if the man was still watching the house. This time, she didn't see him. Suddenly she felt Clayton behind her. He leaned down putting his head right beside hers and gazed out the window.

"What's wrong?"

Should she tell him? Because then he would know she had tried to leave without him. Maybe it wasn't the same man. Maybe she only imagined him.

"Nothing, we better get going. Jeremy hates it when I'm late, because then he has to do the cooking."

Clayton checked his gun and ammunition, and then strapped his gun belt low on his waist. Watching him, her breath became fast and her chest tightened. What was wrong with her? All this after staring at two naked men in the bed. The sight would be with her all day.

"Let's go," he said.

When they opened the door, he stepped out in front of her. "Not to be rude, but this way if someone is going to shoot, I take the first shot."

Stunned, she stared at him. What had she gotten herself into? Never had she really thought about someone wanting to really kill her. She was just a plain girl who struggled to make ends meet.

A cool breeze blew early this morning before the Texas sun would scorch the earth later and yet just thinking about the two men naked in bed had her breathless and warm. Too warm.

Taking her by the arm, Clayton moved her between the building and his side, off the main street. His eyes were the same color as the clear morning sky and his gaze shifted looking everywhere to make certain they were not being followed.

"Don't you think I'll be all right after today?" she asked. "I mean, surely they have moved on to find their treasure."

Yet, she'd just seen the outlaw, Tray, waiting for her across from her home. She had nowhere else to go.

"No," Clayton said. "You could testify against them and then they would hang. Until you're dead, they're going to be searching for you."

His words worried her. She couldn't afford interference in her life. She needed her job to buy food to keep from starving.

"How long is this going to take? We don't even know where to capture them?"

He laid his hand on her arm and squeezed gently. "It's going to be all right. Harley and I will stay with you until they're caught."

Warmth spread through her, and she realized she wanted them with her in her tiny house. Though if the gossips learned of their presence, she would be a ruined woman. But rather ruined than dead.

"That could be weeks or months," she said.

"I don't think so," Clayton reassured her. "These men are not patient and they're going to try something soon. Whatever you do, don't leave without one of us being at your side. Don't go outside after dark alone. If shooting starts, get down. Be very vigilant about your surroundings."

They continued walking down the street and were almost to the restaurant. With a sigh, she closed her eyes for a second "Thank you for protecting me."

She glanced up at Clayton and a smile spread his lips. "My pleasure, Rena. I just wish we had met under not such a stressful event. It would have been better to meet at a church supper."

A grin spread across her face. "Oh, you would not

have come over and spoken to the old maid sitting on the blanket by herself."

"You're wrong," he said. "I would have brought you a bowl of ice cream and even fed it to you."

The very idea of him spoon feeding her the cool sweet had her sighing.

"Who says you're an old maid?"

"Me," she replied, wishing she had never mentioned that word. "I'm twenty years old."

Laughter came from Clayton and he pulled her closer. "I like the fact that you're not some young girl who has no clue about life."

And yet she was clueless about what went on between a man and a woman. Sure, she knew about the act, but how did you get there?

They had arrived at the restaurant. Jeremy was just flipping the sign to open. Was Clayton flirting with her? The thought made her heart pound even harder.

"Are you going to stay and wait for me, or go on to the sheriff's office?"

"I'll have some breakfast and we'll see how things go, but I'm probably going to be right outside the door where you are."

This was going to be tricky. Jeremy was such a stickler about talking to the patrons and not being too flirty. What would he do when she told him that Clayton was her bodyguard?

"I can leave after the noon meal today," she said. "Jeremy likes to keep our hours to a minimum in order to keep from paying us as much."

Clayton swore and she could tell he didn't really like Jeremy much. But he was the boss and at least she wasn't lying at the whorehouse. This job paid just enough to keep her off her back.

"I'm going in through that door right there. You go in the front door," she told him. "I'll see you later."

It was all she could do not to reach up and kiss him on the cheek. Was this how it would feel when someone courted her?

"No, I'll walk you to the back door and then return through the front of the diner."

Taking her by the hand, he led her to the door.

When she walked in, Jeremy frowned at her. "Who's the man?"

"My bodyguard," she said.

"Your what?"

"I witnessed a murder last night. The men are after me. They want to kill me."

Jeremy frowned. "You? Rena Hall? Our little mouse?" Then he threw back his head and laughed. "That story is not going to get you a day off."

"I didn't expect it to," she said, putting her apron around her waist. She looked at the orders that so far Jeremy had taken, ignoring him.

Quickly she got into her routine with cooking, bacon, eggs and even whipped up some biscuit dough and put it in the oven. Then she made the gravy that so many of their clients loved.

Jeremy disappeared and then came back in. "Two more orders."

"Yes, sir," she replied. Every job had things that one didn't like, and she had Jeremy. She was grateful for the job, but he could be an ass. Today she refused to put up with his sass.

Suddenly, the back door was kicked in and she screamed as the man from the night before walked in and grabbed her by the wrist.

"Clayton," she screamed. "Help me."

He hit her across the face, and she kicked him.

The click of a gun had the man freezing. "Let her go or I will enjoy putting a bullet in your skull."

The man shifted her, putting her between him and Clayton.

"You that fella who interrupted us last night in the saloon. This here pretty woman is my wife."

Why did they continue to use that excuse when they all knew it wasn't true?

"Shut the hell up. I know that's not true," Clayton said. "Release her or I'm going to make this kitchen area a bloody mess."

The man moved her slowly to the door. "We're not going to hurt her."

"Just like the murder you committed last night?"

"What murder? She's telling you lies," he responded with an evil grin.

"She didn't tell me," Clayton said and Rena felt the man tense. He had backed to the outside door still swinging with the wind.

"I'm going to find you and you're going to regret being this much trouble for me." With a shove, he pushed her at Clayton and ran out the door. Her protector ran to the open doorway and looked to see where he had gone.

When he turned back to her, she was crying. "He said he's going to find me."

Her big strong savior took her into his arms and held her. Then he lifted her head until she was gazing in his eyes. "He can try, but he's not going to win."

Suddenly his lips covered hers, his mouth commanding and taking control. His tongue slipped between her lips and she moaned as he assaulted her mouth. Rena had never been kissed before and she didn't know if this was normal, but she liked the way he held her head in his hands and controlled her mouth. She liked the warmth flowing through her body, straight to between her legs.

But most of all, she liked Clayton.

"What the hell is the meaning of this?" Jeremy cried. "Who broke the damn door?"

When Clayton released her lips, he smiled at Jeremy. "Rena quits."

"What? No, I can't quit," she cried.

"Yes, you can," Clayton said and took her hand as they stepped through the back door.

"Good," Jeremy cried. "No one else in town will hire you when I tell them what you did."

Clayton stopped, turned, and gazed at the man. "I wouldn't advise you doing that. I'm a Texas Ranger and we're very protective of our women. Now, you have customers you might want to see about."

Rena stood there in shock. She'd just been fired from her job. How in the world would she support herself now?

CHAPTER 7

When Harley came in that evening, Clayton met him at the door. "Rena is furious with me."

"Why?"

"Right after we got to the restaurant this morning, Jack Bell busted down the back door and tried to grab our girl."

"Damn," Harley said. "They're serious."

Clayton then proceeded to tell Harley about how he rescued her and then told her boss she was quitting.

"So why is she mad?"

"Because she has no other income and she's pretty much destitute," Clayton said. In a way, he felt guilty for doing this to Rena, but she couldn't continue to work there with a dangerous criminal after her. In fact, they probably should hole up somewhere other than her home, but he knew a hotel would be out, because she would never sleep in the same room as them. And there was no way she was staying alone.

"I think you should marry her," Harley said.

"No woman, especially a good one, will want to tie themselves to a man whose mother was a whore."

Harley's face darkened and he shook his head. "Damn it, Clayton, I wish you would get over that. You're a fine man. Who cares about you mother or father? It's you the woman should be interested in."

The man didn't understand. He had not been subjected to the bullying and ridicule Clayton faced when growing up. The name calling of his sweet momma, who was only trying to survive. Just like Rena.

"Look, I'm not certain of my future. I, at least, owe my old man a visit, and just as soon as we're done with this case, I'm going to Dallas. You marry Rena and then if things aren't what they seem in Dallas, I'll be returning."

Clayton stared at him. "So, what do we tell her about you? Oh, he's just going to be your part-time husband. That's not how we planned our ranch."

"There's a sweet piece of property up for sale come not far from the Guadalupe River, right outside of Blessing. Two hundred acres. I think we should put an offer on the place and when it's ours, I'll come back for visits."

Harley was the brother he never had. Until he met Harley, he'd never had such a close friend, someone he could depend on. And the thought of him going to Dallas and never returning terrified him. Maybe if they purchased the property and Clayton married Rena, he would have second thoughts.

"You put the money down on the property," Clayton said. "I'll marry Rena if she'll have me. I'm telling you, most people when they learn my background, they want nothing to do with me."

A smile spread across Harley's face. "First, we have to convince her that we're looking out for her best interests. You need to do some major asking for forgiveness. Make her think you were only trying to protect her."

That wouldn't be easy. He'd been trying to calm her, but so far, she was still as angry as a chicken with a wolf in the hen house.

"That's what I've been trying to do all afternoon," he said. "And she's still mad."

Harley opened the door and walked in. The smell of home cooking hit him in the face and he sighed. "That smells heavenly. I'm starving."

"Let's talk to her after dinner tonight," Clayton said.

Ignoring him, Harley went in search of Rena, and Clayton followed. What was the man up to?

When he walked into the kitchen, she turned and gave him a glare as she took the food out of the oven.

"Rena," Harley said in that deep voice that women loved.

After she set the food on the table, he took her in his arms. "Clayton said you had a really bad day."

"Yes," she said. "He got me fired."

"For your own good," Clayton said, walking up behind her and wrapping his arms around her. They had her sandwiched between them, just like they hoped to soon have her. Clayton prayed she would forgive him for getting her fired, but he was only trying to protect her.

A look of surprise crossed her face as she was being held in the arms of both men.

"We're going to protect you and keep you safe," Harley told her. "We're not going to let anything bad happen to you. Clayton was just doing his job. You were in danger at the restaurant."

A tear trickled down her cheek. "But it was money for me to support myself."

Harley reached up and wiped the tear away. "We've got some ideas. Let's eat and then we'll talk about your options."

Her emerald eyes suddenly softened and the fear he'd seen on her face all day disappeared. Just like that, Harley had charmed her and now he needed to do the same.

"Everything is on the table," she said. "Let's eat."

The two of them went outside and washed up, then came back in the house. As they entered, Harley turned and warned him.

"Don't mess this up," Harley told him. "I think she'll agree if we give her all the reasons."

"Which are?"

"She needs us," Harley said with a grin.

Harley was the charmer and he was the one who made the ladies laugh and feel at ease. It was why they were a good team. When they stepped into the kitchen, she sat at the table waiting for them.

"Gentleman, which one of you would like to say the blessing?"

Stunned, they looked at each other. Finally, Harley spoke up. "I'd be happy to."

The smile she bestowed on him made Clayton almost jealous. Someday he hoped she would smile at him that way.

After Harley said the blessing, they dug into the food, and Clayton knew the restaurant had just lost their best cook. And frankly, he didn't care. Because, hopefully, she would soon be cooking for the two of them full time.

Once finished, they helped her clear the dishes away. After scrapping off the plates, she heated water and began to wash.

"I'll dry," Clayton told her.

She glanced at him, and he knew she was still angry. He hoped that tonight would clear away her anger.

"There's something you should know about me," Clayton said, thinking maybe now was the time to tell her about his parentage.

"What? All I know is that you like for women to starve," she said.

If only she knew what it was like living in a brothel. The women were paid very little as most of their earnings went to the madam for food and board. And with a child, the mother paid extra, and that took most of his mother's earnings. Sometimes when the business grew slow, they all sacrificed.

"No, I don't. I've been hungry before. It's not good."

She gave him a sly glance and he could see she was intrigued.

"When did you go hungry?"

"Growing up as a child in the bordello where my mother worked," he said.

Turning from the dishes, she gazed at him. "Your mother worked in a—"

"Yes, and I have no clue who my father is," he said. "Could be any number of the cowboys she entertained."

A look of shock was on her face, and she shook her head. "Oh, the things life teaches us. What was life like growing up in a bordello?"

No one had ever asked him this question, and it made him feel good that she was interested.

"It was different. The ladies were all my mothers. They took care of me until I was about fifteen and then my mother told me she loved me, but it was time for me to leave unless I wanted to work for the bordello. I never saw her after I left. Less than a year later, she died."

It had been heartbreaking when one of the women there had sent him a letter telling him about his mother's death.

Rena was silent as she washed the same dish over and over.

"I think that one is clean," he told her, and she turned to him, then for the first time since they were at the restaurant, she smiled.

"I'm sorry about your mother," she said.

"Yeah, me too. But it's been a while."

Her brows drew together and he could see she wanted to ask a question.

"What were the nights like living there? Did you ever get tired of it? What all did you see?"

He laughed and knew her curiosity was a good thing. Because her interest about what went on in a whorehouse meant that maybe she was a little interested in sex.

"Most nights were quiet, but Friday and Saturday, it was a party house. Men were entertained by the women and then they would disappear upstairs where we would hear the loud moans and the noises coming from the rooms. When I was fifteen, my mother caught me looking through one of the peepholes and that's when she decided I was old enough to leave."

"Peepholes?"

"They are holes in the wall where you can watch people having sex. It's especially interesting if they're doing something kinky."

She licked her lips and quickly rubbed another plate. "What does kinky mean?"

"It means they tied the woman up, or they would spank her, or sometimes two men would take her at the same time," he said, watching her reaction. "Anything sexual that is different."

Her eyes widened and her mouth opened.

Harley, who had gone into the bedroom, returned to the kitchen. "What are you talking about?"

"My childhood," he said, glancing at the man.

"You told her about where you grew up?"

"Yes," he said.

"You're still here. She hasn't kicked you out of the house yet?"

Maybe it was easy for his friend to make light of, but Clayton still worried. This woman was a God-fearing woman who probably worried about being forced to work in a whorehouse.

"Not yet," he said.

Rena took the pan off the stove and began to clean it, at first not responding to his answer. Oh my, was she considering kicking him out?

Suddenly she turned and glared at him, her emerald eyes flashing with irritation. "Why would you think I would turn you out? We cannot control who we are born to or what happens in our lives. All we can do is try to help one another get through this journey."

Stunned at her response, Clayton stared at her. No woman had ever said anything like that to him. For the first time in his life, he felt accepted by a woman.

"You'd be surprised at the people who want nothing to do with me after they learn who I am."

She poured the tub of dirty water down a pipe that

led out into the backyard. "Well, it's not going to be me. You're a good man even though you got me fired."

When she put the tub away, Harley took her by the hands and led her to the table. "We need to talk to you."

"All right," she said.

Clayton joined them at the table, knowing that Harley was going to tell her about their lifestyle and how they enjoyed sharing a woman.

"Clayton and I have been friends for a long time. We have shared being injured, chasing criminals, fighting gun battles, and many lonely nights on the road. We know just about everything there is to know about each other."

Taking a deep breath, Clayton picked up where Harley stopped. "We're tired of being Texas Rangers. Of being alone. We want a family, kids, and a wife that will love both of us. We've even found some property to buy to build a ranch on."

A little jerk came from her. Her emerald eyes grew large, framed by those dark lashes as she gazed at them in a curious way.

"We're looking to purchase some land not far from here and want to start our own cattle ranch," Clayton said even knowing that Harley had not yet decided one hundred percent.

"What do you want from me?" Rena asked. "Are you going to need a good cook?"

A smile crossed Harley's face. "Oh, honey, we want more than just your fabulous cooking. We want you to be our wife."

Her blonde curls tossed about her shoulders. "But I can't marry more than one man."

"You're right," Clayton said. "You would marry one of us, but we would both consider you to be ours. We would both claim you. Any children we have are our children. All we expect from you is to obey us. If you don't obey, then you would be punished."

She glared at him, and he wondered if she would consent to marrying him.

"I'm not a child. I don't need punishment. I would ask for a loyal man who would protect me, shelter our family, and take care of us. Too many times in my life, there has been no one to take care of me."

"We would always take care of you," Harley said. "You never have to worry about working again. As your husbands, it would be our duty to provide for you and our children."

Shaking her head, she stared at them. "Then how would you punish me, because I can tell you right now, I will not accept a man beating me."

"Never," Harley said. Clayton wanted him to talk

about his past, to assure her that she had nothing to fear, but he didn't tell her about his childhood.

"We would spank you if you disobeyed us," Clayton said.

"Spank me?"

"Yes," Harley said. "But we would never harm you or hurt you. But you would be punished."

For a moment, she was silent and then she gazed at each man. "How would you claim me? One at a time?"

A grin spread across Clayton's face. "Oh, honey, at first, we would only take your pussy, but eventually we will also take you in your ass. Now, I know that must sound terrifying, but really it's quite pleasurable."

"All my life, I've dreamed of being in love when I marry. You men don't love me," she said wistfully.

"Not yet," Harley said.

Clayton licked his lips. Oh, he knew he was already falling for her and they had only been together since last night, but there was something about Rena that his heart and soul recognized and wanted.

"Give it time," he said softly, wishing he could promise her hearts and flowers and everything she deserved.

A sigh escaped her, and she gazed at the two men. "I have one condition before I will agree to marrying you."

"What?"

"Can we go to Blessing's whorehouse and look through peepholes that Clayton was telling me about. I want to see what will be done to me. I need to know before I can say yes."

The two men turned and stared at each other. This was the farthest from what he expected. And yet it really sounded exciting.

"Of course," Harley said. "We'll go tomorrow night."

A smile spread across her face. "I can't wait."

CHAPTER 8

Now that Rena was here, she felt nervous. Would her men think it strange that she wanted to witness what it was for two men to take a woman? To see what actually happened in the bedroom.

Last night, she'd been shocked that they asked her to marry them, and yet, it was exactly what she wanted. Since they saved her in the saloon, she'd been dreaming about what it would feel like to be in their arms.

Being with both of them was different and that's why she needed to understand what she was accepting.

As they walked up to the whorehouse, she glanced up at the sign. Her men led her around to the back door and then covered her face with a scarf. They were trying to protect her reputation.

"This way no one will see you," Clayton said. They led her up the steps and into the house.

"Madam Mollie, thank you for having us tonight," Harley said as they came into the rear of the brothel.

The woman dressed in the latest fashion glanced at Rena and then smiled.

"The room is all prepared. When you move the painting, you should find the peepholes. Cherie just went in with two gentlemen. So you need to hurry."

Rena wrung her hands together as she walked past the madam and up the stairs with her gentleman. The lady probably thought they were going to have sex, but they weren't married, so that was not going to happen tonight.

Harley put the key in the lock and entered the room, followed by her and then Clayton. They had shielded her as much as possible from the prying eyes of anyone they met in the hall.

Slowly she removed her scarf and hat. Clayton walked over to the painting on the wall and removed it. Then he took a peek at the other side of the wall.

Moans echoed through the room, the noise coming from next door.

"Let me see," Rena said, eager to witness what she could expect if she accepted their offer. She probably would because what did she have to lose? And her men were so very dream worthy.

They moved aside and she looked through the hole. "Oh," she said as she watched the man fucking the woman from behind. He gripped her hips and was plunging in and out of what appeared to be her pussy. The second man was at the woman's head and his penis was in her mouth. His hands were threaded through her hair, and he held her head as he rocked his cock back and forth in her mouth. She gazed up at him like she was worshipping him.

A loud pop resounded in the room and Rena realized the man behind her had slapped her on the ass.

"Squeeze me," he commanded as he slapped her ass again.

Suddenly Rena felt Harley behind her, pushing into her backside. She could feel his cock pushing against her buttocks.

"What do you see, Rena," Clayton asked.

"The woman has his cock in her mouth and the second man is in her pussy."

The man in front suddenly cried out as he held her head against his crotch. "Oh, Cherie, you suck the best."

She smiled up at him, his member slipping from her mouth. Immediately, her hands went to work on him.

"Give me just a minute, sugar, and I'll be ready to sink my cock in your ass."

Rena glanced at Clayton. "Oh, he's going to put it in her ass."

The man pumping into her pussy, slapped her hard on the ass and then cried out.

Both men had come, and she wondered how they were going to do it again so soon. And would they be able to get it into her ass.

Rena turned to her men to see each rubbing their cock through their pants. Harley asked, "Honey, are you all wet between your legs?"

How did they know?

"Yes," she said.

Clayton said, unbuttoning the front of her dress, "Tonight is all about making you happy."

She wasn't certain how she felt about this until Clayton's fingers slipped inside her dress and found her nipples. With a little twist, he sent spirals of desire slamming into her as she gasped.

"Keep watching," Clayton said, pulling his hands away. "Don't take your eyes off the peephole until we tell you to. If you do, you'll get a spanking."

There he went with the idea of spanking her, and yet it dawned on her that the whore had been hit on the behind. Could it be pleasurable? The woman acted like she enjoyed them smacking her on the butt.

There was only one way to find out.

Placing her face against the wall, she gazed at the three people again. One man now lay under the woman and the second man was behind her. He was rubbing something on his cock.

"Put lots of lotion on it, honey," she told him.

The man on the bottom smacked her on the ass. "Haven't we always taken good care of you."

"Yes, you have," she admitted. "Better than most of my clients. With you, I have an orgasm because you're so good."

Orgasm? She leaned back from the hole. "What's an orgasm?"

"Keep your face to the wall and watch. You'll see."

Well, that was certainly no help.

The man behind the woman leaned in close. "Honey, I'm about to shove my cock so far up your ass, you're going to be screaming when I'm done with you."

The whore glanced back at him and smiled. "Please, fuck me."

"With pleasure," he said as he spread her cheeks and took some kind of cream and rubbed it along her ass, sticking his fingers in her pert little rosebud. Then he placed his cock at the hole and slowly began to enter her ass.

"Yes," the whore cried. "It feels so big inside me. You're filling me up."

"Oh, my," Rena said, feeling breathless. "He put it in her ass and she liked it." She felt more wetness between her legs. What was happening to her?

Harley leaned in close. "Just like we're going to eventually do to you."

Warmth spread through and she leaned back against Harley. "Oh my."

With her gaze still focused in the other room, she watched as the man slide his cock until his hips rested against the woman's cheeks then he said, "I'm in. All the way."

"Now my turn," the man beneath her said. Rena watched with disbelief as he entered her pussy.

The whore moaned. "Oh, yes, please, please, I want to come. I'm stuffed with your big cocks."

"Not yet," the man beneath her said. "Unless you want me to take you over my knee and paddle you good."

Even her men had threatened to spank her if she disobeyed and part of her longed to see what that would feel like.

Harley stood behind her and she could feel his erection through her skirts. With a gasp, she turned and looked at him.

"Eyes on the wall," he told her.

"But you said we would wait," she said with a gulp.

"And we will, but you're going to experience your first orgasm tonight," he said as he shoved his cock against her backside. It was long and hard, and she couldn't imagine it being inside her.

Clayton lifted her skirts and she froze. What were they doing? Fear had her gasping as she felt her bloomers pulled down to mid-thigh.

"Clayton," she said.

"Relax, honey, we're going to make you feel so good. Keep watching," he told her as his fingers suddenly found her center.

Surprise fired through her as she realized they were doing with their fingers what the other men had done to the whore with their cocks.

As much as it frightened her, it also sent a rush of desire cascading through her like a flash fire. She tried to watch the others, but it was hard to concentrate on what was going on when there were fingers everywhere.

"She's dripping," Clayton told Harley. "Our woman likes to watch."

"I'm learning," she gasped as he shoved not one, but two fingers inside her. This was how a cock would feel and already she could see the reason why the woman enjoyed the two men.

"Eyes forward," Harley warned her. "We want you to see her orgasm."

Whatever this orgasm was, they were insistent she learn about it. Just then the woman cried out as the men were taking turns filling her with their cocks. In and out of both her pussy and her ass.

"I'm going to come," the whore cried. "Please, let me come."

The man smacked her on the ass and suddenly her body tensed, the woman screamed as she thrust onto them. Her body vibrating and shaking as she screamed with pleasure.

"Oh, yes," she cried as Rena watched in awe. That was an orgasm?

"Squeeze it, baby, squeeze my cock hard," the man behind her said. "Milk it until it slides out."

Panting, she turned and smiled at him until his cock slid from her ass.

They collapsed onto the bed and she lay between them.

"You boys certainly know how to make a girl feel special. When are you coming back in town?"

"Not for a while," the one who had been on the bottom said.

She gave a pout. "But you're my favorite clients."

Suddenly her men were pulling her away from the peephole. Clayton hung the picture on the wall.

When she turned, they were staring at her like she was dessert.

"Can we watch them again?"

Shaking their heads, they smiled at her. "Time to create our own scene. Time for you to experience your first orgasm."

While it had looked like fun watching someone else, actually doing it made her nervous.

"Step out of your bloomers," Harley commanded.

Clayton helped her and then he brought them to his nose. "Sweet, sweet pussy. But you won't be needing these any longer."

"Why not?"

"Because you're no longer going to wear bloomers or any type of undergarments. You will always be available to us, anytime, anywhere we want to take you."

A knot of nerves appeared in her throat and she had a hard time swallowing. Was this what she wanted? They were handsome as sin and yet what choice did she have?

They led her across the room to the bed.

"Strip," Clayton said.

"But we're waiting," she replied.

"Rena, don't make me have to tell you this again. We're waiting, you're not," Harley said. "Now do as you're told or receive your first spanking."

What the man didn't know was that she had a stubborn streak and she could be ornery if needed, and when he commanded her to do something, the resistant part of her wanted to rebel.

For a moment, she stood there and then Clayton came up behind her. "Let me help you finish with the buttons on your dress." He'd already unfastened half of the them.

"I can do it."

But did she want to?

They watched her and finally she began to unbutton her dress. Slowly letting it slide to the floor, she stood before them in her silk petticoats, lace chemise, and corset.

"Oh no, this has got to go," Clayton said as he whirled her around and began to undo her corset.

"This is what all women wear," she said in protest.

"Not our woman," Harley told her. "We want to walk up behind you, lift your skirt and fuck you. We want to feel your breasts against our hands. We want to see our babies suckling at your breast."

Clayton tossed her corset aside. "Never again. Doesn't that feel better?"

Maybe, but she would never admit it to them. Suddenly she felt her chemise being lifted over her head. Her petticoats were all that were left.

Nervous, she crossed her arms across her breasts trying to hide them.

"No, honey, never hide yourself from us. You're beautiful and we love seeing you naked. I can't wait to taste those sweet breasts," Clayton told her as he moved her arms down.

Harley removed her petticoats and she stood before them naked. They stared and she wondered if they did not approve.

"We are two very lucky men," Harley said with a gasp. "On the bed, honey."

She scooted onto the mattress and Clayton climbed up with her.

"Aren't you going to take your clothes off?" she asked.

"Oh, hell no," he said. "Because then we would not be waiting until tomorrow."

He took her hand and laid it on his cock and she gasped. He was hard. Very hard.

"I did that?"

"Yes," he gasped.

Harley was between her legs, whipping up shaving lather in a mug.

"What are you doing?"

"Hold still and you'll see," he said with a grin.

Suddenly she felt the brush between her legs. A spiral of heat seemed to explode within her as all her nerves came alive.

"Oh, my, what is happening?"

Clayton's lips closed around her breasts and a tingle zipped through her straight to the apex of her legs. Both men were making her feel so very wanted. So very good.

"I'm going to shave you," Harley said, but she no longer cared as all the desire seemed to center between her legs.

"Then I'm going to lick you from top to bottom," he said.

She felt the razor and held her breath hoping he didn't cut something he shouldn't. "Look at that sweet pussy," Harley said.

Unable to resist, she glanced down and saw the lips that outlined her pussy. It was then that she remembered the whore did not have any hair down there.

Harley spread her legs wider as his head disappeared between them. She cried as she felt his lips on her folds. His tongue licked her sending strange sensations through her body.

"What's happening to me?" she asked, her breath rushed.

"Relax," Clayton said "You're about to have your first orgasm."

She remembered the whore and suddenly she understood why her body tensed and her voice called out begging to come.

"Ride it, baby," Clayton said. "Just let your body take over and it will carry you."

Her hands clenched the bed covering and she could feel the tension gripping her. "Oh no. Oh, no. Please."

Clayton's lips covered hers and his mouth was demanding as his tongue swept inside her mouth.

She couldn't breathe.

"Clayton," she cried as she pulled her lips from his, her body arching up off the bed as Harley continued to lick her, the sensations growing.

Her body tensed and her breathing became a gasp for air.

"Harley," she cried.

"Ride it, baby, ride it," he murmured against her.

Then the explosion inside her took her over the edge and she screamed as she closed her eyes. For a moment, she lay there not moving as she slowly ebbed back to earth and her mind recognized that they were still in the whorehouse.

And she had just experienced her first orgasm.

When she opened her eyes, her two men were

staring at her with the biggest smiles on their faces. But there was more and suddenly she wanted it all.

"Why are we waiting?" she asked. "What was it that whore said? Fuck me, please, fuck me," she said with a gasp.

The two men immediately shook their head. "Not until we're married. But we do have something for you," Harley said.

He held up a spiral shaped wooden dowel.

"This is a butt plug. Since I had the pleasure of eating your pussy, Clayton is going to show you how it works and put it in. Every few days, we'll give you a bigger one until the day that your ass is property stretched and prepared."

She stared at the dowel. "Won't it hurt?"

"A little, but we're going to make it pleasurable. You're going to have your second orgasm of the night," Clayton said, taking it from Harley and putting lotion on it just like the man in the other room did for the whore before he put his cock in her ass. "Up on your knees."

It seemed like such an awkward and embarrassing position to be in.

"Someday soon, we're going to take you just like those two men took that whore in the next room."

At the mere thought of two men fucking her, she felt

herself growing wet again. When she was up on her knees, Harley ran his hand over her buttocks.

"Man, I can't wait to give you a spanking," he said.

"No, it will hurt," she whimpered.

"But it will also feel good," he said as he popped her on the ass.

Stunned, she felt the heat spread from her buttocks to her center, her pussy clenching, looking for something. Was she a bad girl if she enjoyed what they were doing to her body? Did all married couples do this?

He smacked her again and she moaned as she felt his fingers rubbing between her legs, stroking her clit. In the past, she had touched herself, but this was much better.

"Oh," she cried.

"Keep doing what you're doing," Clayton told Harley. "She's enjoying it. Look at that sweet little puckered rosebud. I can't wait to sink my cock inside you."

She licked her lips and then she felt a finger slowly rubbing circles around her ass.

"Lean down on your arms, baby," Harley said.

When she did, she felt Clayton's finger go inside her ass and she froze. It didn't hurt, in fact, it felt good. Gently he pushed in and out and she wanted to grasp his finger and hold it there while Harley rubbed her clit.

Between the two of them, they were driving her over the edge once again.

"I think she likes this. She's gripping my fingers."

"Put it in," she said, knowing the feel would send her into orgasm.

Clayton removed his fingers and she felt the wooden dowel. It stretched her and she gasped at the width, but he continued. When it was firmly in, he began to pull it out and she cried out.

"Oh, Clayton, please," she cried as her body flooded with heat.

He hit her on the ass and that sent her over the edge once again.

"Fuck me," she screamed just like the whore, and now more than ever, she understood why she was begging the men to stick their cocks in her. Never had she felt so much.

While her body slowly relaxed, she felt the butt plug in her ass, still there as a reminder. Every move she made would make her long for her men's attention. Every move would remind her that soon they would claim her back there.

"How am I to work with that thing up my ass? It's going to make me want the both of you."

"And that's why we did it," Harley said.

They grinned.

Clayton got down on one knee. "Now, will you marry us?"

How could she deny them when she wanted to experience more of this pleasure?

"Yes," she gasped.

"Come, it's time to go home. Tomorrow is our wedding night," Harley said, rising from the bed.

Clayton held out his hand to help her up. "You are a very hot, passionate woman and I can't wait to make you our wife."

They handed her dress to her. "That's all you need. The rest of this will be discarded."

The thought of walking through town naked except for her dress had her cringing. Why did she get the feeling this was going to be a new way of life? One she would have to adjust to.

CHAPTER 9

Rena was sleeping like the dead when a torch flew through her window. Glass sprinkled her as the burning stick landed on the floor between the bed and dresser.

With a gasp, she sat straight up on the mattress and screamed. Jumping out of bed, she picked up the torch and flung it back through the window then tried to smother the flames with a quilt from the bed.

The cracking of a second window had her running into the main area of the house. "Harley, Clayton, we're under attack."

A bullet whizzed by her ear and she drop to her knees. The second torch was burning and she picked it up and quickly put out the fire it started by beating it with a rug.

Clayton ran into the room, bare chested, pants barely up, his Colt 45 in hand, and fired out the broken window. The man's looks were tossed with sleep and all she could think about was he would soon be her husband.

While she could hear Harley in the bedroom cursing as he fired from his window, she wondered how he looked.

Crawling to Clayton, she handed him the torch and he threw it out into the yard as he fired another round of bullets at a shadowy figure climbing onto a horse. They heard two horses gallop away.

It was over.

Rena sat in the floor, trembling. If they had lost the house to fire, she would've been destitute with no place to live. The few family heirlooms she possessed would be gone, and she would be without a home and a job.

Clayton knelt beside her. "You all right?"

"No, why is this happening to me? Where would I live if this house burned down?"

"With us," Harley said. "As our wife."

The memories from earlier in the night came flooding back. They were to marry tomorrow, and it dawned on her that as their wife, she would go where they went. This house, this home, she could possibly never live here again. And while that made her sad, it also was intriguing. She'd never lived anywhere but here.

"Where are we going to live if not here?"

Clayton glanced at Harley and it was a look of frustration. "We're going to stay here until I can purchase our ranch. Then we'll build our home and settle in with a couple of babies."

Children. Oh my goodness, what would they tell their young ones?

"How will we explain us to our children?"

"We're going to tell them we lead a different kind of life and that we're very happy."

Stunned, she continued staring at them. They made everything seem so logical, but she knew that it couldn't be this easy. And yet, she had willingly spread her legs for them earlier tonight. For a woman who never even courted one man, she wanted to experience two men at once.

"Do you think I'm a bad girl because of what I did with you tonight?"

Both men started laughing.

"Well, do you?" she demanded.

"Hell no. In fact, we're so happy that you like sex and we think we'll be very happy," Clayton said.

Glancing around at the damage, she looked at the

windows. "Three broken windows are not going to be cheap."

How would she pay for them? How could she continue not to work when marauders were trying to burn down her home?

"No, it's not," Harley said. "And we need them boarded up."

"We'll pay for them," Clayton said. "You've been feeding us. Your money is running low, so we'll fix the windows."

Grateful, she stared at him. Was this what it would be like when they were married?

Harley nodded. "Since Clayton got you fired, he should be the one to fix them."

"Hey," he said. "You're eating her food as well as me."

Harley laughed. "But I was trying to put it off on you."

The two men were cracking jokes at one another right after they had been under another attack. How could she continue with this man determined to kill her? How could she sleep with the windows now broken?

"You should sleep with us tonight," Clayton said. "There is not a good way to protect you. They could slip in a broken window."

The man read her mind. And the thought of going back into that room and sleeping alone terrified her. A chill spiraled up her spine. By the time they realized she was gone, Jack Bell could have her out of town. Yes, she would sleep with them tonight.

"I don't think they'll return tonight, and if we all sleep together, then everyone is safe," Harley said.

Sitting on the floor, she realized she was in her nightgown, but then again, they had already seen everything.

"If you don't marry me tomorrow, I'm a ruined woman," she said as she slowly rose to her feet. It was true, after what they had experienced tonight, sleeping in the same bed couldn't be any worse.

Harley checked the doors. He put a piece of furniture over the window in the main room and nailed a bed slat across the window. They weren't getting in tonight.

Then they all went to the men's bedroom and she crawled in bed. Each man lay on either side of her and a feeling of safety and security filled her. Would this be how their nights were spent?

This was where she belonged. Between her two men. Protected. And tomorrow they would marry her and claim her for their own.

"Good-night, gentlemen," she said.

"Good-night," Clayton replied as he laid an arm around her.

"Good-night," Harley said. "Tomorrow night we won't get much sleep, so we better catch some shut eye while we can."

"I can't wait," Rena said as she turned over and her eyes closed. "Sex with my men."

CHAPTER 10

Whatever reservations Harley had about marrying Rena were gone after the time they spent in the brothel last night. The way she cuddled in her sleep. The warmth of her, the sweetness that oozed from her as she did her best to help them repair the house. The way she had worn her best dress to marry them, without her underclothes.

"Let's stop by the sheriff's office before we head to the church," Clayton said, pulling his bolo tie straight.

Harley had worn his best shirt and pants. All of them were cleaned up and looking like they were on their way to a party instead of a wedding.

"We need to tell him about last night's attack," Harley said. "And that we're marrying Rena."

A blush spread across Rena's face as she gazed at them. "Everyone will know what we're going to do tonight."

The men laughed. "They'll be thinking those guys are so lucky."

"No, they'll be thinking Clayton is the lucky one," she said.

And it suddenly hit Harley that Clayton would be the legal husband. He would be the one no one knew about.

As much as Harley wanted to marry Rena, it was best she married Clayton since his own future was so uncertain. After she told Clayton his mother raised a good man, it eased his fears. But Harley wasn't certain of their future. As much as he wanted to stay and be Rena's other husband, he had to settle with his father first.

He wasn't sure if he would stay. And he couldn't tell her just yet.

"Is everyone ready?" Rena asked.

She looked gorgeous in a blue dress that fit her curves without anything extra beneath. With her blonde hair and emerald eyes, he knew they were going to be two very lucky men to have her in their life.

"Let's get married," Clayton said with a grin.

"Yes, let's get to the church before he closes. I can't wait another night," Harley said, remembering the feel of her body snug against his own last night. The taste of her on his lips, the way she curled around his body in her sleep and how he couldn't wait to sink his cock deep into her.

They walked out the door and Harley carefully looked up and down the street. Then they pulled her out, carefully locking it behind them before heading toward town.

It wasn't far and soon they entered the sheriff's office. Harley noticed a woman with a baby in her lap sitting in his office.

"Oh, sorry, you're busy," Clayton said as they walked in the door.

"No, this is my wife Lillian," Seth said. "She was in town and decided to wait on me. That's our son Will."

Rena, like all other women, was drawn to the child. "Oh, he's growing so quickly."

"Yes," the woman said. "And we have a second one on the way. Very soon. Your dress is so pretty. Is something special going on?"

"We're getting married," Rena said with a smile.

The sheriff and her men all looked at her.

"Congratulations," the sheriff said.

"Oh, how wonderful," Lillian said and then she frowned. "Which one are you marrying?"

"Clayton," she said smiling.

The sheriff glanced between the two of them. "Wait a minute. I know what you are doing. The same as me and Will. You're going to share her."

Rena's head dropped and Harley felt bad about embarrassing her.

Lillian's fingers lifted her head. "Do not be ashamed. I'm married to two wonderful men who have taken such great care of our little family."

Rena's emerald eyes widened and she glanced at her men. "There are other married couples like us."

The men smiled at her. "Yes, there are."

"Soon we need to all get together. We're a community now."

Lillian leaned over and whispered something in Rena's ear and her eyes widened. She smiled. "Thank you. I'll remember that."

"Oh no, the women are plotting against you," the sheriff said.

Harley shook his head. "Last night, we had two armed horsemen throw torches through the windows and fired shots into the house. Luckily none of us were hurt. They took off before I could see their faces."

The sheriff sighed. "I've been doing some follow up and talking to the neighbors. One said they did hear screams that night of the killing. Why in the world they didn't check them out, I don't know, but they did hear some yelling."

Harley stepped back. "Have you heard anything else about the missing map?"

"No, that's a dead end."

They glanced at the women quietly talking. The two had a common bond and Harley could see that Lillian was indeed making Rena feel calmer about wedding and committing to the both of them.

But could he commit to her? And if he didn't, would she realize that he had not promised to love and stay with her forever? Yes, he wanted a family. Children and a wife to love, but first, he had to meet with his father. How could he find peace if he didn't go to him?

"It's three o'clock and if we're going to get married and then have dinner at the restaurant, we better get a move on," Clayton said. "But we wanted you to know the killer has not given up."

"Be careful tonight," the sheriff said. "But most of all, I hope you have a wonderful wedding and fantastic wedding night."

Harley glanced at Rena and her cheeks flushed pink.

"I told you everyone will think about it," she said as she looked at Harley.

"Who cares?" he said. "All that matters is what happens between the three of us."

"You're going to be a married woman," Lillian told her as she squeezed her hand.

Harley glanced at Clayton. It was time to make Rena theirs. Even if he didn't stay, he knew he would always be welcome if he decided to return. Or at least, he hoped he would.

CHAPTER 11

As they were walking home from the cafe after a nice dinner, Rena had never felt more nervous. She would've thought after everything that happened last night, she would no longer have wedding night jitters, but that wasn't true. Already she could feel herself becoming attached to her husbands, and while she wanted them both, she didn't want to disappoint them.

What if she was lousy at having sex? That whore last night had seemed so at ease with what was going on and Rena didn't feel like that at all.

The whore seemed to be in control in some ways, by teasing and giving the men pleasure. Rena felt no control. All she felt was fear.

"Are you wearing the butt plug?" Harley asked her.

"Yes," she said in a whisper, afraid someone would hear him. This was all so new to her and she still felt uneasy about having not one, but two, men. In some ways, she felt greedy, but she would look at them and think *they're mine*.

"What did you enjoy the most about last night?" Harley asked.

She thought for a moment, and she could not deny it. "When Clayton put the butt plug in. It shocked me to feel so much desire when he touched me back there. And I imagined you beneath me and Clayton at the back, just like the whore in the next room."

Now they would tell her how ashamed they were of her. Tell her she must be a whore if that's what she enjoyed, because it was not where she expected to find pleasure.

"I liked when you licked me, but the way Clayton prepped me for the butt plug, that was something."

Crickets sang their lonely song as the sun slowly sank below the horizon. She kept waiting for them to shame her, but they didn't say a word.

"Aren't you going to tell me I'm bad?"

"No," Clayton said. "Honey, we are here to make you feel good. And if that's what excites you, then we're going to do more of it. We're all about pleasuring you. And in return, we hope you will do the same for us."

Harley picked up her hand and squeezed it. "I can't wait for you to suck my cock."

Could she do that? Sure, she'd seen the whore do it, but could she put his dick in her mouth and suck on it?

"And I can't wait to slide my cock into your sweet pussy," Clayton said.

They walked up to the front of the house and Clayton swung her up into his arms and carried her across the threshold.

"For good luck," he said as he let her slide down his body. His cock was hard, pressing into her. Soon she would be experiencing that cock inside her and a shiver rippled through her.

"Are you cold?"

"No," she said, wishing they would hurry.

Harley moved up behind her and they had her sandwiched between them. "Go into the bedroom and prepare yourself. Be on the bed, naked, with your head on your arms and your ass sticking up in the air."

She swallowed nervous and yet eager to touch their bodies. Tonight was the night. Soon, she would no longer be a virgin. She would no longer be an innocent.

When she went into the bedroom, the stubborn part

of her resisted climbing onto the bed and waiting for them. As she removed her clothes, she didn't want to be on her knees. She wanted to see their bodies. She longed to touch their cocks with her fingers.

With a sigh, she crawled on the bed and put herself in the position they requested.

A few minutes later, they entered the room, and she heard the sounds of their clothes dropping. Then they approached the bed and she flipped over onto her back.

"That's not what we told you to do," Harley said.

"How can I see your bodies, your cocks, if I'm on my knees with my head on my arms? I've waited a long time to experience a cock between my legs and I want to see what I'm getting."

Clayton started to laugh. "She has a good point."

Their abdomen muscles were strong and rippled, their waists narrow, and their cocks jutted out from their bodies, strong and defiant. They placed their hands on their cocks and moved the skin back and forth.

"Have you seen enough?"

"No, but it will do for now."

Staring up at them, she frowned. "Is this going to hurt?"

"Honey, did you enjoy last night?" Clayton asked her. They were married. He was her husband.

"Yes," she said, remembering the things they did to her. The butt plug that was still inside her. But tonight, they would claim her. They would take her virginity and suddenly she felt afraid. "Maybe we need more time."

She stared at their cocks and knew somehow they'd fit inside her body, but how?

Part of her wanted it done now, and the other part was frightened, and the thought of them putting their cocks inside her scared her.

Harley's mouth came down over hers, effectively shutting her up. As his lips moved over hers, Clayton kissed her neck, her back, his tongue trailing along her spine sending delicious shivers through her.

They flipped her over, once again in the position they desired.

The kiss that Harley bestowed on her had her clinging to him, his lips consuming hers, his tongue sweeping the inside of her mouth as fire raced through her and she wanted more. Oh, how she wanted and needed more from her two husbands.

As he kissed her, her nerves seemed to settle, and in their place, a hunger began to build.

When Harley broke the kiss, she didn't want him to stop. A growing heat blazed between her legs as she stared into his brown eyes, feeling like she was swirling out of control.

"As your husbands, we want you to want us as much as we can hardly wait to get inside you. If you're not begging us to take you, then we haven't done our job," Clayton whispered. "I'm very confident you're going to soon be begging me or Harley to put our cocks in you."

Confusion swirled inside her brain. They wanted her to beg them to take her? Even the whore had not begged, though she did scream *fuck me*. Was that considered begging?

His lips covered hers again and Clayton continued his assault on her senses as his tongue trailed all the way down her spine, reaching her derriere. Then he pulled apart her buttocks and blew on that most private of spots, sending a swirling tornado through her all the way to her cunny.

"Clayton," she gasped, breaking the kiss with Harley.

Already they had introduced her to how good it felt to have her ass massaged and even to have that wooden dowel put inside her.

Sensations whirled through her as they rolled her onto her back and Harley moved his mouth to her breasts, sending tingles straight to her center. A moan escaped from her lips.

Then she felt Clayton spread her legs and look at her in the most intimate of places.

"Oh, Harley, you're right, she's got the sweetest little pussy. And it's my turn to taste it."

As he spread her innermost lips and placed his mouth on her center and kissed her, shockwaves of pleasure pulsed through her. Last night, Harley had kissed her in her most intimate spot and she had loved how he made her feel. Tonight, it was Clayton's turn and the way he shoved his tongue inside her had her gripping the sheets of the bed.

"We're going to taste you in every way. And if we do it right, you're going to scream with pleasure."

A whimper escaped her as Harley placed his mouth on her nipples, sucking them into his mouth and nipping at the hard pebbles. Just like yesterday, pressure was building inside her. Only today, she spread her legs wider, feeling decadent, giving Clayton even more access, wanting to feel that rush of desire that would take her over the edge.

"Don't stop," she moaned, knowing she was so close.

Slap! His hand found her pussy and he slapped it hard enough to send tingles radiating through her.

Slap!

"Never forget that we are in control, especially in the bedroom. You don't tell us what to do. We are your men," Clayton said as he slapped her pussy one more time before his fingers found her clit as he tweaked it gently.

As her essence coated his digits, his fingers toyed with her. An urge to offer him even more of her body had her raising her hips.

"I think she likes having her pussy spanked," Clayton said.

"Slap it again," Harley said, rising from her breasts.

Smack!

Her body tensed as she was sucked into a vortex of pure unadulterated lust. Yes, they were married, but she needed more from him.

"Please," she said. "Fuck me."

What was she saying? Was she really ready for him to take her maidenhood? He said she would be begging and she was.

Her body tensed and she lifted her pussy as high as she could to let him shove his fingers deeper. Suddenly an explosion of light and color surrounded her as she screamed.

"That's it, honey," Harley said. "Come for us."

She clinched Clayton's fingers as he slid them inside her and she screamed her pleasure, the sound echoing in the room. Her breathing was fast and quick and yet she knew she wanted more. Needed more.

Slowly, the world seemed to right itself and she gasped

as Clayton stood and lay on the bed on the other side of her. Once again, she was sandwiched between her men, and she liked the feel of their hard bodies surrounding hers.

"You like having your pussy spanked. I could tell," Clayton said. "I think I'll do that again soon."

What was she supposed to say? When he spanked her pussy, a rush of heat consumed her. Would they think she was a wanton? Was she?

With a sigh, she quietly said, "Yes. I did."

They pulled her into an embrace between them.

"Good. We enjoy spanking you and we love to see you come. Whatever you enjoy is not wrong between the three of us," Harley said. "Now, I'm going to take your virginity. Be prepared for it to hurt just a little, but once it's gone, it will never hurt again."

Harley rolled onto his back and Clayton lifted her and placed the entrance to her cunny on top of his cock. She glanced down at the size and fear filled her.

"I don't know. Harley, you're so big."

"Relax and soon you'll be having another orgasm."

While that sounded wonderful, it was getting his cock inside that frightened her.

Rising a little, Harley kissed her again on the lips, nibbling at her bottom lip. Heat began to swirl inside her once again.

With Clayton's help, she sank a little lower onto his cock and then she felt him entering, stretching, and filling her. For a moment, she didn't dare move, but then he gave a little shove and she felt the membrane give from the pressure.

"Aargh," she cried.

"Wait, it will go away, I promise," Harley said soothing her.

Clayton found her clit and began to rub it, sparking her pleasure once again.

A gasp escaped her as she slid the rest of the way down to sit on his stomach.

"Oh, she is so tight," Harley groaned. "Her pussy is clenching around my cock."

"Don't come unless we give you permission."

"But why?"

"Because we said so," Harley said with a groan.

Clayton moved behind her and kissed along her neck, whispering in her ear. "Now you belong to us. Never forget you're our wife. You're ours. Soon we'll take you at the same time."

For a moment, it felt awkward as she rose and slid down his cock, but then the friction between them began. The slide of him going in and out of her wet pussy made her moan as she felt her muscles tightening around his cock. Pleasure had her breathing rapid and fast.

She was stuffed with Harley's cock in her pussy and she couldn't imagine taking a cock in her ass at the same time. There was no room, or was there?

Heat flooded her body as Harley's hands tugged and pinched her nipples. With a moan, she closed her eyes and let her head roll back.

"Look at me, Rena. We're in this together and I want to watch your expression when you explode with passion. When my seed coats the walls of your womb, I want to be gazing into your beautiful eyes when we create our child."

Gazing at Harley, her breathing was harsh as she felt Clayton pulling on the butt plug, plunging it in and out, rubbing his finger at her back entrance. How could something so depraved feel so good? She'd never imagined such pleasure.

"Don't come," Harley demanded.

How was she supposed to stop the rush of heat filling her, flooding her, and making her want to desperately find release?

"Hold on," he said. "I'm almost there."

She groaned and it was all she could do not to scream with frustration. Her body was shaking as she held the orgasm at bay, so ready to go spiraling over the edge.

"Now," Harley said.

It was then that Clayton's hand landed on her ass, the butt plug buried deep inside her and she screamed as her body convulsed. Panting, she never imagined what Harley said would be true. That she would loudly proclaim her pleasure.

Drained, she slumped onto Harley's strong chest, knowing she had made one of the best decisions of her life: marrying her husbands.

"My turn, Rena. Watching you and Harley, I can't wait to come inside your pussy."

Yes, she wanted to experience Clayton. She wanted to know how his cock would feel filling her. Would he give her the same pleasure?

"I'm so ready. This is going to be hard and fast."

What did he mean by hard and fast? He rolled her onto her back and pulled her to the edge of the bed. Lifting her hips, he lined up his cock with her cunny. In one fluid movement, he slid inside her.

"Damn," he said. "Harley was right, you are so tight."

Lifting her legs, he spread her wide as he sank deep inside her. Suddenly he was pounding his cock into her pussy over and over again, fast and hard. Once again, the pressure was mounting inside her and she clenched his cock.

After having come twice, she was shocked at how once again her body responded, her muscles clenching and gripping him.

"Oh, Harley, my seed is racing us toward the finish. Rena is perfect for us."

Harley chuckled and leaned down and kissed her on the lips. The feel of his mouth on hers, the way his tongue glided over her lips and slipped between them, sent fire coursing through her body. Each man was intent on giving her pleasure.

Each thrust took her closer and closer to the edge. Gripping the sheets, she could feel another orgasm building. She lifted her hips to meet his thrusts wanting as much of him as she could take. Needing him deep inside her.

Each man felt different. Each man's cock gave her pleasure and she knew she was about to come.

"Please, may I come," she gasped between breaths, knowing she couldn't hold out much longer.

"Yes," Clayton said. "Come now."

This time the explosion raced through her, sending her spiraling out of control. Screaming, she grabbed the sheets to hold on while Harley held her in his arms, rocking her. Clayton stared into her eyes and she felt like they were one.

With a grunt, his seed flooded the walls of her pussy. He continued to hold her legs up as they both tried to regain their breath.

"Let's hope tonight we created a baby. A girl with your looks or a boy to carry our name."

Oh, yes, she would love if she became pregnant tonight. And already she knew she was falling in love with her men. Two men. Her men and she was their wife.

When Clayton rolled over, his hand came into contact with Rena's sweet flesh. A surge of happiness filled him as he woke to Rena draped across his body. Last night, they slept only a few hours, spending most the of the time exploring each other's bodies. Still, he felt rested enough to want his new wife again.

Staring down at her, blonde hair draped across his chest, he knew he would do whatever it took to protect her. They had to catch the killers in order to keep Rena safe. And starting today, he and Harley had to focus their days on the hunt and their nights on Rena.

It wasn't until he met Harley and they shared a prostitute that he considered the idea of sharing a woman. But now they had a wife, and Clayton couldn't wait to get her with child. He wanted children. A baby suckling at her breast. A toddler running through the house. Children playing outside.

A normal family. And he hoped and prayed to God that Rena was truthful with him when she said she had no problems accepting a whore's son. Because he wanted his children to have a normal life. One with two fathers and a mother. Maybe it was a little strange, but he would always be involved in his children's lives. Always.

Harley stirred and rolled toward their woman.

"Did we fuck all night?" he said softly. "I don't think I've fucked that much since I was a young man."

Clayton laughed. "Yes, and I think we should start out the morning that way as well."

The thought of them taking her together was enough to make him hard again. Yes, they would take it slow, but soon, she would be ready.

"I'm going to wake her up," Harley said as he laid his mouth over hers, consuming her lips as Clayton watched.

Clayton laid his hand on her pussy and began to stroke her clit. Her eyes flew open and she moaned, wrapping her hands around Harley's head, holding his mouth to hers.

Slowly, he broke the kiss.

"Good morning, my husbands," she said softly, arching her back. "Didn't you get enough?"

"Never," Harley said. "Roll over. Up on your elbows with your ass sticking up in the air."

Slowly she moved, her emerald eyes glazed with passion. The sight of her eager and willing to have sex with her husbands warmed Clayton's heart in ways he didn't know how to explain. It wasn't love, but oh my, he would move mountains to experience that passion.

"You're going to fuck me again?"

Harley smacked her on the ass. "Get used to being awakened this way every morning."

Clayton continued to stroke her, knowing they were preparing her for her second butt plug. She was ready, and soon, they would both be claiming her at the same time.

"Every morning, Harley and I will awaken you with kisses and fucking. Every night we will put you to sleep with kisses and fucking."

"And you, my husbands, will have me pregnant in days," she said with a smile that turned into a moan.

Harley crawled out of the bed.

"Don't leave yet," she cried.

Clayton laughed as he continued to stroke her clit watching the desire overcome her.

"He'll be back."

Her hips began to undulate inviting him to shove his hard cock in her shorn pussy. Oh, how he was so ready.

Harley went to his saddle bags and pulled out the tools he needed. Grabbing a jar of ointment, Clayton watched as Harley spread it over the next plug, preparing it for Rena.

Clayton moved her over him, his cock hard and ready as it slipped into her wet and willing pussy.

A gasp escaped her as Clayton's cock moved within her. Harley moved behind her and spread her ass cheeks. Her head whipped around to gaze at him, her breath rushing out.

"What are you doing?"

He held up the plug and showed it to her. "You're ready for the next butt plug. When we reach the fourth, you will be ready for us."

Slowly Harley pulled out the first one, spinning it as she moaned and pushed her ass back toward him. He rubbed some of the ointment on her puckered hole and began to push the pointed plug into her sphincter.

She tensed, and at Harley's nod, Clayton slapped her on the ass sending a ricocheting effect through their bodies all the way to his cock buried deep inside her.

A moan escaped her and Clayton knew that when he popped her ass, it increased her excitement, and like a flower, she slowly opened for Harley.

"Deep breaths, baby," Clayton said, gazing into her emerald eyes. She began to move her hips and when she did, Harley slipped the rest of the plug into her.

"Harley," she cried. "I'm so full."

Clayton leaned in again and pinched her nipples. "Just how you will be with our two cocks in you at the same time."

A moan escaped from her and she rocked back and forth with Clayton pumping into her. Already she gazed at him like a cat in heat. Like she wanted more.

"Oh, Clayton," she cried as he pummeled her pussy, his face tightening as he held onto her hips, pounding her.

Clayton couldn't wait until they both had her at the same time. Then he and Harley would be fucking her and spilling their seed into her.

Twisting her nipples, her moans increased and he knew she was close.

"Clayton," she moaned.

He shoved into her wet pussy and slapped her ass. Just the sounds of their fucking were making Clayton so hard, he feared he would explode before he had the chance to experience her once again.

"Come with me," Clayton groaned as he held her hips tightly and plunged into her soaking pussy.

A scream tore from her mouth as her body

convulsed and she pushed her ass out for Harley's attention. He twisted the butt plug and she screamed as the orgasm overcame her.

"Ohhh."

Before she could come down completely from her climax, Harley took Clayton's position. Rising from the bed, he slipped behind her. Once again, he slapped her wet pussy, reigniting the nerve centered there and then plunged his cock into her.

"Harley," she screamed.

"Fuck me," he told her, and she raised her ass higher allowing him to go deeper.

He thumped the plug in her ass and she moaned as he shoved his cock into her. Rough, not gentle, he gripped her hips, shoving into her cunny as he drove his cock home, pounding into her.

The rush of his seed had him wishing he could last longer. "Who do you belong to?" he gasped.

"You and Clayton," she moaned. "You're my men. My husbands."

"That's right and you better never forget it," he said as he popped her ass with his hand.

"Harley," she cried.

"Come for me, baby," he said as he pushed one last time into her cunt. "Come now."

With a scream, her body squeezed his cock, wringing

every last drop of his come from him. She convulsed with the passion they created as he collapsed on top of her.

"Oh, what a great way to start the day," Clayton said with a sigh as they all three lay on the bed.

Rena laughed. "I'm so glad you got me fired. By now, I would have been at the restaurant working. Instead I'm lying here in bed with my husbands."

CHAPTER 13

*H*arley had never been so attached to a woman. Never. The man who wanted to capture Rena and kill her, he would tear limb from limb if he took her. She was their woman, and while he still felt uncertain about the future, there was one thing he was certain of. Rena.

The woman had a stubborn streak, but overall, she obeyed them and enjoyed having sex. She was open to learning about what gave them pleasure and he could hardly wait to show her how to suck his cock. The very thought of her lips around his shaft had him achingly hard once again.

It was almost noon. After they fucked again this morning, they had taken a bath with all three of them in her small tub. That had led to them bending her over the tub and each one fucking her again.

Afterward, she had dressed and made them breakfast. Harley wanted to have her remove her dress, but what if Jack Bell showed up and she was naked?

A slow burning rage simmered inside him at the thought of this man trying to harm Rena.

"Harley, you're frowning," Rena said. "Are the pancakes not good?"

A slight smile spread across his face. "They're delicious, but I'd rather lay you on this table, pour syrup on you and lick it off."

A blush spread across her face. "Later."

He liked the fact that she didn't tell him no, but rather *later*. And the idea of her naked and spread with sweet syrup flowing on her body was something he was looking forward to.

Clayton smiled. "Too hell with later, I say we do it right now."

Rena squealed and suddenly stood. "Boys, it's late."

"Who the hell cares what time it is?" Harley said. "It's never too late or too early to have you spread beneath us."

The sound of knocking came from the front door and the two men frowned. While Harley didn't think that Jack and Tray would knock on the door, you just never knew how brazen some criminals could be.

"You expecting anyone?"

"No," she said nervously.

Harley was not going to take a chance. "Clayton, go to the window and look out. I'll go to the door. Rena, you get to the bedroom and stay there."

While they all scattered to their positions, Harley walked to the door.

"It's the sheriff," Clayton hollered.

With a yank, Harley opened the door. "What's up, Sheriff?"

"We need to talk. I waited as late as I could before I came to see you."

"Come on in," Clayton told him. "We just finished breakfast."

Rena peeked around the door. "Can I come out?"

The men frowned but nodded.

"Have a seat, Sheriff," Harley said.

The three men gathered in the main room and Harley knew something had happened.

"What's wrong?"

"Even though I warned him, Leon Roberts was found murdered this morning. Strung up and tortured much the same way as Rena described the body we have yet to find. The inside of his house had been ransacked like they were looking for the map. If he had it, it's no longer there."

If they had not located the map, Harley knew the criminals were still in the area searching. If they had found it, they were on their way to find the silver.

"Anyone see or hear anything?"

"No, his neighbors have that deer in the lantern light look, so if they heard anything they're not talking."

These men were cold-blooded killers. To torture someone to death was the cruelest way to die. If the map was in the house, he would have told them when the pain became so excruciating that he couldn't stand it. Or if he had given it to someone, he would have told them.

"That map is not in that house," Clayton said, shaking his head.

"Agree," said the sheriff.

"Why do I feel like we're at a dead end? At least we have Leon's body, but what can that tell us other than the fact that they are savages?"

The three men sighed.

"Go talk to Granny Bailey," Rena said, walking into the room. "She has lived in Blessing all her life. From the time the community was formed. She knows the families and if there was a map to a silver mine, I bet she knows who has it or if it even existed."

The woman was trying to help but listening to an

old woman's gossip wouldn't help them. Harley didn't care if they never found the map, as long as they found the two men on the killing spree before they reached Rena.

"The men aren't staying in a hotel," the sheriff said. "They must be holed up somewhere out of town. I thought that tomorrow we could get a group of men together and search for them."

Harley glanced at Clayton and knew he was thinking the same thing. What would they do with Rena? They couldn't leave her here alone.

"Could Rena stay with your wife out at the ranch? You've got plenty of protection there, right?" Harley asked.

"Of course, Lillian would love to visit with her. She's almost nine months pregnant, so she's not getting around much right now."

"No," Rena said out loud startling the men. "There is so much work that needs to be done around here. I'm going to stay home and work."

Harley didn't say a word and neither did Clayton. Like hell, she was going to stay here by herself with that demented killer searching for her. If he had to strap her down on his horse, she would be going out to visit Lillian.

The sheriff stood and smiled at them. "I'll see you

men in the morning about six thirty. Maybe we can find their hide out."

Clayton walked the sheriff to the door and closed it quietly. Then they both turned to glare at Rena.

"What?" she said. "I need to do laundry, clean the house, and cook dinner. I don't have time to go out to Lillian's. I'd love to visit her, but I just don't have time."

Harley walked over to her and knew she was going to receive her first spanking of their marriage.

"You are never to disagree or argue with us in front of company," he said. "You just earned your first punishment spanking."

Her mouth fell open and she licked her lips nervously. "I was just telling you my thoughts."

"And you think we're going to go off and leave you alone with a madman looking for you, wanting to kill you?" Clayton said. "Go to the bedroom, take off your dress, and wait for us."

"It's time we punished you," Harley said, anger rising inside him at how she had disrespected them.

CHAPTER 14

Well, damn! Rena knew the moment she said the words, the glances they gave her, told her they were upset. But a spanking? An honest to goodness punishment. She liked it when they were making her excited by hitting her pussy or her buttocks lightly, but somehow she feared this was going to be worse.

For a moment, she sank down onto the bed. Why were they going to ruin what they had together? Why would they hurt her because she had expressed her opinion? This could be a problem in their marriage if every time she disagreed they punished her. Nothing would stop her from expression her opinion. She was going to speak her mind.

Suddenly they were in the doorway and she had not removed her dress.

"You haven't taken your dress off," Harley said in an angry tone. "That's another strike."

"No, I wanted to understand what I've done that is so bad," she said. "All I did was tell you that I don't want to go to their house."

Why could they not understand that a woman's work was never done and there was so much she needed to do to make this place a good home for her men.

"All we ask of you is to obey us," Clayton said. "You are our wife and your safety is our concern. We want to make certain you are well taken care of. Tomorrow, we both need to be searching for this outlaw. If you stay with Lillian, we will be certain of your safety," Clayton said.

Well darn! They were thinking of her safety and she was thinking of their comfort.

The expression on Harley's face was not good. And she knew she had crossed the line.

"Because I said so," Harley told her.

"If you're home alone, we'll not be concentrating on our jobs and that puts us in danger. We need to know you are safe while we hunt for this killer," Clayton said.

That was not how she planned on spending her day, but it appeared that her husbands were worried about her safety. And she never wanted to be the distraction that caused one of them to be harmed or killed. She had no choice but to do what they asked of her.

The two men stood staring at her.

"All right, I'll go," she said. "But I would prefer not to receive a spanking."

"Take your dress off or I'm going to rip it off you," Clayton commanded, and she knew they were losing patience with her.

With a sigh, she stood and began to unbuttoned the front of her dress. Slowly she removed it, not wanting this to happen too quickly. Since they didn't allow her to wear underwear, there was no way she could drag this out. The muslin dropped to the floor and she stood naked before them.

Harley sank down on the bed. "Over my lap."

"You're not going to hurt me?"

"We will never harm you, but you will be punished," Clayton said. "Punishment never feels good."

With a sigh, she lay across Harley's lap. Her stomach over his legs.

"What are you being punished for?"

"Not wanting to do what you asked me to do," she said.

"Also for disagreeing with us in front of a guest," Harley said.

His palm connected with her ass.

Slap!

"Count," he told her.

"One," she said, determined not to cry, though her buttocks stung and it was only the first one. "How many are you going to give me?"

"That's for me to decide. You will accept however many I give you," he told her.

That didn't sound good.

Slap!

"Two," she said, gritting her teeth as warmth spread across her upturned cheeks.

Smack!

"Three," she groaned.

Slap!

"Four," she said, trying not to think about the pain that now radiated from her buttocks.

Smack!

For a moment, she had to catch her breath when the pain became intense.

"Five," she gasped, tears flowing down her cheeks. At this moment, she almost hated him for what he was doing to her.

Harley rubbed his hand over her buttocks in a soothing way.

"Next time, obey us and we won't have to do this

again," Clayton said, gripping her pussy and stroking her clit.

Heat seemed to expand from her buttocks all the way up through her body, making her limp. Why was she feeling this way? Why did she want them when they had just spanked her hard? Even now, her buttocks were enflamed with heat.

Harley raised her off his lap and laid her on the bed. She watched as he began to remove his clothes. They were going to fuck her. Even after punishing her. That didn't seem fair. She didn't want them and yet, she did.

Tears pooled in her eyes.

"What's wrong, honey," he asked.

"You hurt me," she said. "My buttocks hurt."

"And now we're going to make you feel better," Clayton said. "Don't cry. It's only because we care about you and want you to be safe. We don't like punishing you."

"Yes, you do," she said with a sniff.

Clayton removed his clothes and then crawled up on the bed and took her in his arms. "If something happened to you, we would feel like it was our fault for not protecting you."

"You are very headstrong," Harley told her. "You're used to doing things your way. Now it's going to be our way."

"But what if I object. Don't I get a say?"

"Of course, you do," Clayton said. "We'll listen to your wants and needs, but then we will have the final decision."

Part of her wanted to scream in frustration at the idea of surrendering everything to them. She was, after all, a human being with wants and needs.

"Just realize that when I want something, I'm going to fight for it," she told them. "I wanted a day to work around the house. Be alone. Make this into a home where my men were comfortable."

They smiled at her.

"You're tired of us already?" Harley asked.

There were so many feelings rushing up inside of her. "No, but I haven't had a day to myself to work in the house in a long time. It just sounded so nice."

"And you'll have one, just as soon as we catch these criminals," Clayton assured her, kissing her cheek. His lips wound their way down her neck. Tingles started in her center and spun their way back up her spine.

"Are you still mad at us," Harley asked as his fingers found her center and he began to tweak her clit.

She sniffed. "A little. My cheeks are burning."

"Let me make them better," Clayton said as he flipped her over onto her stomach.

She felt his hands massaging her cheeks and then his

mouth was on her buttocks as he kissed her white orbs before his lips found her little rosebud.

"Aw, darling, I can't wait to take you here," he said as he twirled the butt plug inside her, sending waves of heat undulating through her body. She gasped at the sensations that were flooding her. A moan escaped.

"Open your mouth, Rena," Harley said.

Flicking her eyes upward, she glanced up to see his cock right in front of her face. He wanted her to put it in her mouth just like she'd seen the whore do. What would it feel like? Taste like?

With a swipe of her tongue over her lips, she opened her mouth and he put his cock on her mouth. Gradually he pushed it inside.

"Suck and lick it," he told her.

As she tried to concentrate on the large growing member in her mouth, Clayton continued to stimulate her from behind. It was hard to think straight when he had his fingers shoved inside her pussy, thumping on the butt plug that impaled her.

The ache disappeared from her buttocks and was replaced with a growing need for someone to stick their cock inside her.

With her hand, she pulled Harley's cock from her mouth.

"Clayton, please," she cried.

"What do you want?" he asked.

"Put your cock in me. Fuck me," she said and realized that the whore had used the same words and now she understood why. Now she was the one crying out in desperation for them to satisfy this want inside her.

Knowing that she wanted to please Harley, she put his cock back in and began to suck even harder.

"Damn, Rena, for a first timer, you know how to suck a man's cock," he said and shoved it in farther.

Her throat seemed to open and she could feel his cock down inside and she had to fight to keep from gagging.

"That's it, honey," he crooned to her. "Keep sucking. I'm about to come and I'm going to fill your mouth with my come. Swallow it."

Harley shoved his cock deeper still and she felt her throat flooded with his come. He gave a final shove, holding her mouth to his crotch and then he was pulling out of her throat.

"Good job," he said as he reached down and kissed her on the mouth, his tongue swirling inside.

Needing air, she pulled back and gasped. "Clayton, please, I want to come."

"Not yet," he told her. "Don't come unless you want me to spank your pussy."

Now that didn't sound bad. But she held back,

fighting to control the urge to let go and come. Suddenly she felt his cock sliding into her pussy as she clenched onto him, wanting him deeper.

"Oh, yes," she said.

A rhythm began to build between them as he shoved his cock in her and she slid back to meet him partway.

Just when she was about to come. He stopped.

"No," she cried.

"Are you still mad at us," he asked.

"I'm going to be furious if you don't finish fucking me," she said.

Slap! His hand landed on her pussy and it just made her need even greater.

"Beg me," he told her.

What did he want her to say? A craving unlike anything she'd ever felt before filled her and she only wanted his cock buried inside her.

"Take me. Make me yours. Fuck me deep and hard," she gasped.

Lifting her hips, he held her as he fucked her hard and deep, just like she requested, and she met every thrust squeezing his cock.

Gasping, he slapped her lightly on the buttocks. "You may come anytime."

And she did. Clenching down onto his cock, she screamed as the orgasm took her and carried her away.

She gasped as she felt his seed coat the walls of her pussy. As she drifted down to earth, she couldn't help but wonder how it could get any better.

Even when she was angry with them, they still made her feel so very good.

CHAPTER 15

Rena's buttocks were sore as she bounced around on the saddle. Clayton had insisted she ride a horse to Lillian Parker's home. Since she had only ridden on a horse three times in her life, she felt a little nervous. But he swore she was going to become quite proficient at handling a horse.

"Every rancher's wife knows how to ride a horse," Clayton said. "And soon so will you. I'll even buy you a horse."

Not something she wanted, but if it made her husband happy, then she would gladly accept his gift.

They were pushing her beyond her boundaries and making her learn new things. In some ways it was helpful, but dang, if it wasn't nerve-racking sitting atop a huge animal trying to give it directions.

Thankfully, her horse followed Harley's mare and all Rena had to do was hang on.

When they stopped in front of Will and Lillian Parker's ranch that they shared with Sheriff Seth Ingram, they were all outside waiting.

"Good morning," they called.

In the distance, Rena could see men working the horses and the cattle. Someday this was what her men wanted. A cattle ranch. And while she would hate leaving her childhood home, it was time. The old house needed a lot of repairs, and it would be good to start somewhere fresh.

Harley helped her down from the horse.

"You're going to be good and spend the day with Lillian," he said.

"Well, I'm not going to ride the horse back alone," she said with a sigh. "Yes, I'll be waiting for the two of you when you return."

Clayton shook his head, pulled her to him and then swatted her on the ass as he whispered in her ear. "Don't make us have to spank you again."

She frowned up into his face but didn't say anything.

"Are you ready to go?" Harley asked the sheriff.

"Yes," he said. "Will is going to help us out. He used to be a Texas Ranger as well. Now he's a cattleman."

Rena watched as first one man and then the other

kissed their very pregnant wife while she held their eighteen-month-old son.

Harley turned to Rena. "Stay with Lillian."

He kissed her on the mouth and then popped her on the ass. "Don't make me punish you again."

With a sigh, she turned to Clayton. "Be careful."

After a brush of his lips against hers, he walked away and climbed upon his horse.

The four men rode off and Rena strode toward Lillian. While she really enjoyed spending time with her, there were so many things at home she'd wanted to do. Maybe Lillian could tell her about living with her two men.

"I hope that I'm not a bother to you today," she said.

"No, in fact, I could use the company. The men can be so demanding and I see yours are as well. Let's go in the house and I'll fix us a glass of tea."

As they walked inside the house, Rena couldn't help but admire the rich furnishings. Lillian put the baby down and he hurried off to play with his toys scattered about the main room.

"Watch out for toys," she said. "When you have children, you'll understand that your house will never be the same. Toys everywhere."

"Did the men tell you where they were going today?" Rena asked, curious about which direction they were headed. As it was, if they didn't return, how could she send out a search team for them?

Lillian shook her head. "No, all they said was that they were going to search to see if they could find where these two men were hiding out. You will soon learn that lawmen are always in protective mode."

"Tell me about it," Rena said. "I wanted to stay home, clean the house, and make a nice dinner for them tonight, but they became angry about me disobeying them."

With a smile, Lillian laughed. "I know what you mean. We women are for their pleasure. Have your men taken you at the same time yet?"

Rena felt her face blush.

"You are so innocent," Lillian said. "From the expression on your face, I can tell they haven't. Just wait. It's going to be so great. You're going to enjoy having sex with them at the same time."

Uncomfortable, Rena didn't respond. "Do you find this life awkward with two husbands?"

"No, it's the best thing that ever happened to me," she said. "And now with our second baby on the way, I'm so happy. Soon you'll have your own little one."

In some ways that thrilled her, yet, she was still so new at being married to not one, but two, men that she wanted time with her husbands to become accustomed to them both. To learn how to handle marriage with two men.

"When is your baby due?" Rena asked.

"Any day now. If our calculations are correct, he's due next week, but I expect him or her any day now. I'd really like to have a girl this time, but I know my husbands want another boy. Just a healthy, happy baby would be great."

She didn't want to frighten Lillian and tell her that her mother died from complications of childbirth. Her baby brother died along with her mother.

The baby came running over to Lillian and she sank down onto a chair and pulled him into her lap. "We're such lucky women to have two men who love and want to protect us. I can't imagine not living with both of my men. Don't you feel the same?"

As much as she was struggling, it was hard for Rena to say that she cared as much as she did.

"Last night, they spanked me hard for not wanting to come over here. So I've been a little upset with them. They made me sore."

Lillian smiled at her. "They were probably looking out for your best interest."

It was true, but Rena did not want to admit just how much she feared the Red Jack Gang. She'd seen what they were capable of—cold-blooded murder.

"It's so hard for me to let them take control. No one has ever done that for me."

Lillian frowned. "What do you know about their backgrounds? That could have something to do with why they were so strict on you."

If only. "No, I think they were hard on me because they think I'm stubborn."

Laughter spilled through the room. "What woman isn't? Do you know their pasts?"

"I know Clayton's, but I know nothing about Harley. He's very quiet. He's a little hard with his mannerisms, but yet, there is a sweet, soft side to him as well."

The baby curled up in Lillian's lap and she knew he must be wanting a nap.

"You need to learn his background because that will help you understand him. We all have things in our past that we'd rather not face, but once we do, those things are healed. When you get him in bed tonight, ask him about this past."

Now that she thought about it, it was odd that Harley had said nothing. And she didn't think he had even promised her that he would stay forever.

"Did Seth promise you forever?"

"Of course," Lillian told her. "Both of my men promised to stay with me. One was a civil ceremony and

Seth told me that even though our vows were not legal, I was his wife, just as much as Will's. Why do you ask?"

"Because Harley has never promised me anything. And he's been rather quiet about what he expects from me."

"You should ask him," Lillian said. "There must be a reason."

A trickle of misgiving scurried up Rena's spine. Harley had said nothing. No promises. Nothing. Why?

They had ridden in ever widening circles around the town of Blessing and found nothing. Wherever the Red Jack Gang were hiding, it was a good location.

"What now?" Will asked as they rode back into Blessing.

"Let's go see Granny Bailey," Harley said, remembering Rena's advice. What could it hurt to ask the older woman about the map? If it had a history, maybe she would know.

"Why?" Seth asked. "She's almost ninety."

"And she knows the history of the town," Harley said. Yes, he was ready to go back to the Parker ranch and pick up Rena, but first he wanted to ask this older woman some questions. Maybe she could tell them something that would be the clue they needed.

"The woman is a tough one. She's been married twice and the last husband was ten years younger than her. She's outlived them all," Will said. "Maybe she would know something."

They rode up to her house where she lived with her son who ran the mercantile. They climbed off their horses and hurried up the steps.

When they knocked, a servant answered. "We'd like to talk with Granny Bailey," Harley said.

"Just a moment," the woman replied. "Let me see if she's up to seeing visitors."

A few minutes later, the woman hurried back to the door. "Come into the parlor. She'll join you in a moment."

As they walked into the small room, Harley couldn't help but notice the tintype photos of two men. He peered at one.

The woman walked into the room as silent as a woman with a cane could.

"Husband number one. Bill Bailey. A rotten man who gave me my two sons and the other one is George Jones, a good man who left me way too early."

Harley frowned. Something wasn't right. "Why are you called Granny Bailey and not Granny Jones."

A grin spread across her face. "Because everyone in town knows of my son's store and they all called me Granny Bailey. What can I do for you, gentlemen?"

Using a cane, she hobbled to a chair and sat. "These old bones don't let me stand too long."

Harley couldn't imagine being almost ninety and wasn't certain he wanted to find out. "There is a man killing people in town who he believes has a treasure map. Since you've lived here for a long time, we wondered if you knew anything about the families who had the map."

The woman cackled. "That map has caused problems for over sixty years. It always brings out the greediest of men. Yes, I can tell you about the map since my father originally owned it."

Harley stared at the woman. Rena had been right.

"My father stole the silver from Jean Lafitte and hid it somewhere on the Guadalupe River. He drew a map that showed the exact location, but then knowing that Mr. Lafitte would come after him, he hid the map. Only Jean Lafitte didn't come after the silver; he sent henchmen to kill my father. Eventually they were successful. Papa died in a gun battle, but they never came after the silver.

"Two years later, a man by the name of Frank Griffin stole the map from my brother's son. What Frank didn't know is that we had searched all along where the silver is supposed to be and it's gone. We looked the entire area over and found nothing. It's either buried very well or the landmarks have changed or someone found it."

"Frank's wife said he hasn't been home in a week. She fears something has happened," Seth replied.

Could Frank be the man that Rena saw killed? He had to be an older gentleman.

"What about Leon Roberts? How does he play into this?"

The older woman gave a chuckle. "Leon wanted to be rich. So when Frank got into a financial bind, he purchased the map from Frank. Damn fool knew there was no silver on Guadalupe River."

"I think Frank and Leon are both dead," Seth said. "We haven't found Frank's body, but I know Leon is dead. He was murdered."

"Do you know a man named Jack Bell?"

The woman rolled her eyes. "Oh, yes, he's from the wrong side of the family. He's my great-nephew. He's part of the Red Jack Gang."

"Yes," Harley said. "Have you seen him?"

"I'd shoot him if I did," she said. "That boy is nothing but trouble. He grew up on tales of our family stealing that silver from Jean Lafitte and had big dreams of finding it and becoming rich."

Harley knew they had hit a gold mine of information.

"Would he kill to find his dream?"

A cackle came from between the woman's dry lips. "Oh yes. He'd kill you just to empty your pockets."

Clayton stepped forward, leaned down, and stared at the older woman. "Who do you think has the map now? It wasn't found in Leon's house. We don't think the killers have it. Where can we locate the map?"

"That, sonny, is the biggest question of all. Who has the map?" A grin spread across her face. "Leon did not have it."

Harley knew. "You have the map."

She smiled. "It's a family heirloom. The silver that my father buried and no one can find even with the map is not there. The map is useless. The treasure cannot be found."

And he'd bet that she knew what happened to the silver. No, she had the map. She just refused to tell the law officers that it was safely hidden somewhere in her home.

"Do you know what happened to the silver?"

"No, I do not," she said with a smile that Harley did not believe.

The servant walked in.

"Mrs. Jones, it's time for your supper," she said.

The woman smiled at the gentlemen. "Is there anything else I can help you with? If not, it's time for me to eat, and at my age, you never know when a meal is going to be your last."

The men watched as she rose from the chair and walked them to the door. When they reached it, she waited. "Gentlemen, I hope you find the men you're searching for. Kill that bastard Jack. He's been worthless all his life and has brought nothing but disgrace on this family."

With that, she turned and walked to the kitchen while they filed out of the house. Harley wanted to ask Rena some questions about the man she saw. He must have been an older gentleman to have stolen the map from the son of Granny Bailey's brother.

CHAPTER 17

Clayton was disturbed when they got home that night. Granny Bailey had the map, but she was not going to admit that she had the piece of paper that her great-nephew was killing for. One family in a small town could cause so much trouble.

When they arrived at the ranch, Rena had been taking care of the baby while Lillian had lain down to rest. Her time was drawing near and she'd been exhausted. So she napped while Rena cared for baby Will.

He'd been proud of her for not attempting to leave before they came back. Though he could see that she was tired. They were all exhausted after spending half the night fucking. In fact, they'd done nothing but that the entire two days they'd been married.

Clayton helped Rena down from her horse and then went inside with her while Harley took care of the horses.

As soon as they were in the house, Rena turned on him. "Why did Harley not commit to our union? Lillian told me that both of her men made vows. Seth made her a promise that he would be with her forever."

This was what Clayton had been dreading. Rena was not a dumb woman and after talking to Lillian she realized something was wrong and it wasn't Clayton's place to say.

"You need to talk to Harley about this," he said.

"You know, don't you? He hasn't even told me about his family. You told me about your mother and growing up in a whorehouse. But Harley has said nothing. What is going on?"

If only Harley had told her the truth at the beginning. But now she was suspicious and there was nothing he could say. Maybe he could distract her.

"By the way, you were right about Granny Bailey. We visited her this afternoon. We gleaned a lot of information from her. Enough that we may be able to soon catch these men. One of the men we're searching for is her great-nephew."

"What?"

"Yes, Jack Bell is her nephew."

Rena walked into the house and set her satchel down. "I'm glad you learned some information while visiting her. I also learned a lot about a marriage like ours from Lillian."

She reached up and stroked Clayton's face. "Thank you for being honest with me."

What could he say? He couldn't tell her Harley's secrets. Those were his to confess and yet he agreed with her. And he could tell Rena was not happy with Harley.

Just then Harley came in the door. "I need to talk to you," he said to Rena.

Clayton felt relief. Maybe now he would tell her about his family. Tell her how he felt the need to go home and make certain his father was all right. Think about taking that ridiculous bribe his father offered.

"Good, I need to talk to you as well," Rena said. "You go first."

Did Harley not see that she had just laid a trap for him. If he didn't come clean now, she was going to let him know her feelings. Let him see just how angry she was with him.

"That first night, when you saw the man hanging in the tree, was he an older gentleman?"

Rena's face seemed to wilt for a moment before she

replied. "It was dark, but I think the man had gray hair. He was large and had a big belly. Why?"

Harley was not picking up on the way she appeared stiff, almost angry at him. Could he not see that he needed to be honest with her?

"We believe Granny Bailey figured out who he was," he said.

"Frank Griffin," Clayton told her, knowing that she needed to be assured that they were both still committed to her and show that they trusted her. "Did you know him?"

"Not personally, but I believe he knew my father," she said.

"What did you want to ask me?" Harley said.

Clayton's insides tightened and he wondered if Harley would be truthful.

Her lips pressed into a line and he could see the flash of anger in her emerald eyes. "Sit down."

The way she said the words, Harley's brows drew together, and he was starting to understand that something had upset her.

Rena took the chair across from him. "Today, Lillian and I were talking and she told me that both of her men committed to her in marriage. Even though Seth is not a legal husband, he told her that he would always be there for her. That he was just as much her husband as Will. It made me realize you never said anything like that to me. Why?"

Clayton could see that Harley was nervous.

"You also have never told me about your family," she said. "Clayton was honest about his."

"You've never told us much about your family," Clayton said, hoping to diffuse some of her anger.

She whipped around to stare at Clayton. "You're right and I should. But first I need to know why Harley is not committed to us. Specifically to me."

Now it was up to Harley to be truthful with her or Clayton would step in. There was no way he was going to lose Rena because Harley hadn't made up his mind.

"My father destroyed our family life. He beat my mother so badly that she eventually died. And the sheriff looked the other way because there were kids that needed taking care of. But he also abused us. A day didn't go by that if one of us slipped up, he wouldn't knock us around. His fists were his favorite tools. The older we became, the more he liked to taunt us, and one day, I'd had enough of being beat. I turned on him and let him experience how my fists felt. He kicked me out of the house and told me never to come back."

Rena stared at Harley.

"Even now, I fear losing control and using my fists. When I spanked you the other night, I had to back down and take a deep breath to keep from really hurting you. It's like that's what I think I'm supposed to do when someone disrespects or disobeys me. That's not the kind of man I want to be."

With a sigh, she seemed to shrink back from Harley. "Are you afraid of hurting me?"

"No, because Clayton would stop me. He's saved me many times. It's like there is a beast inside me, and when I become enraged, he comes out. It's all the anger from my childhood."

Standing, she walked across the room, her hands gripped together. Though he was being honest about his family, he had not told her why he had not committed to her. Pacing the room, she stopped in front of him.

"Do you not want to be my husband? Do you not find me attractive enough to spend a lifetime with me and Clayton? Why can you not commit to me?"

Harley shook his head. "You're beautiful. I'd be lucky to have you for my wife and I do think of you as my woman. But there are some things I must take care of before I can commit to anyone."

Oh, Clayton wanted to hit him. That was not the right thing to say to Rena. He could see her face flush with anger. The woman had given herself to both of them and only one man had been committed to her. Couldn't he see how that would affect her?

"Didn't you think I should know this before we went down to the church and said wedding vows? Didn't you think before I let you sleep with me that I deserved to know this? I thought you were my husband, possibly the father of my child, and now I'm learning you're not even certain you want to remain in our marriage."

Harley looked at Clayton and he shook his head. No, it wasn't for him to defend his friend. He'd brought all of this on himself.

"My father is offering me ten thousand dollars to come home and run his mercantile store. That's a lot of money and I'm tempted to see if he's changed, and if he'll really pay me is a big question. As much as I hate him, he's still my father. If I decide to stay in Dallas and run the store, I didn't want to hold you and Clayton back from finding another man."

Oh, wrong thing to say again.

"What?" Rena said enraged. "Do you think I'm going to let just any man come into our marriage? If you died, possibly, but as far as I'm concerned, you are my husband. And if you didn't want to be in this union, you should have said something before I married Clayton. I could be expecting a child. Your child. And what am I supposed to tell that child? Sorry, Papa went home to Dallas and never returned."

Harley swallowed. "Rena, please give me some time. I

don't know what I want to do. But I have to go to Dallas and see my father. It's been years since he kicked me out of the house. Maybe he's changed."

Men like Harley's father never changed. They only died. But he knew that Harley had prayed to have a family like everyone else. So he couldn't say anything.

"When are you leaving?"

"Just as soon as we capture these criminals, who, thanks to you, we have a clearer understanding of," he said.

The man was trying to get on her good side, but Rena was having none of it.

"I'm sleeping in my bedroom tonight. Because you weren't honest with me, Harley, the two of you can take the guest room."

With a whirl of skirts, she turned and walked away.

"You should have told her sooner. She's really hurt."

"I know, but what could I say? Let me fuck you until I visit my father."

Clayton sighed. Men like Harley were rough around the edges. Not being raised by a women, he did not know how to charm a lady nor the importance of seeing her side and not thinking about only himself.

"There are other ways you could have told her that would have helped her understand. Now neither one of is going to get any pussy anytime soon."

CHAPTER 18

Rena tossed and turned all night in her empty bed. She'd cried herself to sleep so disheartened by how Harley had treated their union. No, he didn't like to be disrespected, but he thought nothing of disrespecting her.

She missed being between her two handsome men. She missed their cuddles and how Harley had a slight snore and Clayton would sometimes talk in his sleep. She missed them fucking her.

When she did sleep, her dreams were weird and frightening with Granny Bailey right there in front of her laughing at her. The woman was almost ninety.

Finally, unable to stay in bed any longer, she rose, had a bath, and took her time preparing herself for the day. Normally, she would have fixed her men breakfast, but today, they could find their own food if they were hungry.

Right now, she doubted that she would fix their dinner either. They needed to learn not to show her dishonor. In a marriage, it went both ways, and she couldn't spank them, but they could go hungry.

When she walked out into the parlor area, she noticed that she was alone. Earlier she'd heard one of them leave, but she didn't expect for them to go off and let her be alone. After spanking her for wanting to stay home, this made her even angrier. With a madman trying to capture her, they left her alone?

A knock resounded on the door and she glanced out the window at a young boy standing there.

She opened the door. "Yes?"

"I was asked to deliver this to you," he said.

"Thank you," she said and closed the door.

When she opened the note, she was surprised.

Rena, I've gone into labor. Could you watch little Will while the midwife delivers the baby. There is a carriage waiting outside for you.

Lillian

What an honor that her friend had invited her to watch her son and be there at the birth of her child. Glancing around, she grabbed her satchel and headed out the door. She didn't know where her men had gone to, but they could find her. She left the note from Lillian on the table, hoping they would see it.

When she walked out the door of the house, a carriage was there for her with a driver she didn't recognize.

"Are you taking me to the Parker ranch?"

"Yes, ma'am," he said.

Not thinking twice, she opened the coach door and crawled inside. Suddenly the vehicle took off and she had to hold onto the seat to keep from falling.

"Oh, dear," she said, thinking that Lillian needed to know how fast her driver drove the carriage. Maybe it was because he wanted to get her to the ranch as quickly as possible. She just hoped they arrived in one piece.

Looking out the window, she realized that she didn't recognize the way the driver was headed. Maybe it was a shortcut.

Thirty minutes later, the carriage came to a halt. She waited for the man to open the door. Glancing outside, she didn't see any buildings.

This wasn't the ranch.

Oh my God, Lillian wasn't in labor. She'd been tricked.

Fear gripped her chest just as the door of the carriage flew open.

A man put his head inside and grinned at her, Jack

Bell, the man who had tried to capture her twice, smiled. "Welcome to hell."

She pulled back not wanting to get out of the carriage. The man was a killer and she had walked right into his hands.

He reached in, grabbed her arm, and pulled her screaming from the carriage with her hitting him with her satchel. "Clayton will kill you. My husband will hunt you down."

The man slapped her, almost knocking her to the ground, causing stars to swim before her eyes.

"Good, that's what I want. I want him to bring me the map to save you. Of course, he won't be saving you. Because I'll kill all of you. That silver is mine and I'm going to find it."

"The silver is gone," she said.

"Shut up. It's there and I'm going to find it," he yelled at her.

Another man came up behind her, grabbed her wrists and tied her hands together. Then they led her inside their camp.

Quickly, Jack wrote out a note and gave it to the other outlaw.

"Post this on their door while they're out searching for her. By now, they must realize she's gone. And we have her."

Fear squeezed her chest. Her men would come, and this fiend would try to kill them. As angry as she'd been last night, she realized the reason was because she loved them. Terror seized her. She loved them both and the thought of Harley lying to her and leaving hurt her so bad. Now they might never have the chance to make up.

And she needed them both. They were her men. Her husbands even if Harley didn't acknowledge that she was his wife.

Tray Lander jumped on his horse and rode off, leaving the carriage behind.

"Now, it's just the two of us. What should we do while he's gone?"

Terror raced through her. No, he wouldn't hurt her yet, would he?

CHAPTER 19

Out in the barn, Harley retreated there to give Rena some space while Clayton worked with the sheriff in town. After last night, he really needed to think about what he wanted. What had his father ever done for him? Nothing except make him meaner and tougher than a man should be.

With Rena, he had been gentler than he'd ever been with a woman. And yes, he thought of her as his wife, but he wanted to be certain before he told her he was committed to her for life. But he'd never thought about her being pregnant as he rode away.

No woman had ever treated him like Rena. She accepted his faults, and he'd done nothing but hurt her. Last night, he'd heard her crying and started to go to her, but Clayton told him to leave her alone. If he wasn't ready to commit, it'd only make it worse.

Even his best friend was furious with him.

The memory of his mother as a gentle woman who accepted her fate rode him hard. Never would he beat his wife. All his life, he'd promised himself he would be a good father. Never would he hit his child in anger. There were other ways of making a child behave and he wanted his son or daughter to respect him, admire him, and be proud of the father he was to them.

That's all he wanted from his wife as well. Someone who adored and looked up to him, to take care of them. He would be their man for life, and he wanted to be certain.

But the thought of leaving Rena possibly pregnant was making his chest ache. How many times had his own father ridden away for days on end, only to return and make their lives miserable once again?

A noise outside the barn drew his attention. The doors to the house were locked and he would hear anyone who came up. Rena was safe while he tried to fix a shelf she adored to make her happy with him again.

He glanced out the window and saw a carriage driving away really fast. A tremor of unease trickled down his spine and he walked out of the barn and to the house.

"Rena," he cried as he walked inside. Glancing around, it was silent.

Yanking open her bedroom door, he saw where she had bathed and cleaned up. He looked around for her satchel. It was gone. Racing back into the parlor area, he called again.

"Rena," he cried.

Nothing.

Angry, he went into the kitchen. If she wasn't answering him because she was upset, he was going to be furious.

Not a sign she had even been in the kitchen this morning. He checked the other rooms in the house and realized she was gone.

The memory of the carriage had fear seizing his chest.

As he walked by a table next to the door, he saw the note.

Picking it up, he read it.

"Fuck," he yelled.

Grabbing his hat and his guns, he ran out of the house, saddled his horse, and rode like the devil was chasing him down the street. When he reached the sheriff's office, Seth and Clayton were in a serious conversation.

"We found the body," Seth said.

"Is Lillian in labor?"

Seth frowned. "Not that I know of. Why?"

He showed him the note. "Rena's missing."

Clayton jumped up. "What? How the hell did you let her get away?"

"I was in the barn. I was working on that broken shelf trying to repair it to make her not be angry any longer at me. While I was there, I heard a carriage pull away and saw it leave. She must have been inside."

Shaking his head, Seth sighed. "If Lillian was in labor, one of the servants would have been here to get me. Plus, Will is there and he would have sent someone."

"Let's go. We need to see if we can find that carriage," Clayton said.

"I should have stayed in the house with her. But I was trying to give us both some distance to get over our argument last night."

The three men ran out the door. "What about tracks?" Harley said, grasping at anything that would find his woman. And she was his woman. His wife. She was his and he'd kill the son of a bitch who took her.

"Too many wagons in town," Seth said.

"What direction was the carriage headed?" Clayton asked.

"West. Let's go back to the house and see if we can

pick up the trail," Harley said, needing to find something that would lead them to her.

Climbing onto their horses, they rode hard back to Rena's home.

When they pulled up, a note hung on the door.

Bring the map by tomorrow morning or she's a dead woman. Meet us at the Guadalupe River near the hanging tree.

Clayton was studying the tracks in the dirt. "Son of a bitch must have taken something and cleared them. I don't see any carriage tracks."

"We've got to get that map from Granny Bailey," Harley said. "No choice."

"How the hell are we supposed to get the map from that old woman?" Clayton asked. "You know she has it."

"All we can do is try," Seth said. "Let's see what we can do."

Harley felt like a piece of his heart was missing as they climbed back up on their horses and headed into town. Once again, he'd messed up his relationship with Rena. Now, he prayed she was safe until they could reach her.

If not, how could he live with himself? What his father had done to him was horrible, but this was ten times worse than a beating.

And he'd kill the son of a bitch who took her if he harmed her in any way.

158

The sun was beginning to sink as the three men stood on the doorstep of the old woman's home and knocked.

Her servant answered the door. "Yes."

The woman did not look nearly as friendly as the day before. In fact, she seemed nervous.

"It's urgent we speak to Granny Bailey," Seth said. "This is official business."

"Come into the parlor and I'll bring her out," she said. "She's not having a good day, gentlemen."

What did the servant mean?

The three men stood in the parlor where they had been the day before. Would she give up the map? Had Harley and Clayton misconstrued her meanings.

The old woman shuffled into the parlor.

"Good evening, gentlemen. What do I owe the pleasure?"

Clayton hoped she would give him the map. "This morning my wife was taken by Jack Bell and Tray Lander. The ransom they are asking for her is the map. From what you said the yesterday, I thought you might have it."

The woman sighed and shook her head. "I'm sorry. I don't know what map you're talking about. A city map?"

"You acted like you were the one with the map for the silver your father stole from Jean Lafitte. You told us it was a family heirloom."

She gazed at them. "I don't know what you're talking about. Map? A map to where?"

Clayton was starting to lose his patience and he knew he couldn't. Rena's life depended on him finding that diagram.

"Remember, you told us your father took the silver from Jean Lafitte and hid it somewhere along the Guadalupe River. You had a map that would lead us to the silver."

"Jack Bell is going to kill my wife Rena if we don't bring the map tomorrow morning to the hangman's tree on the bank of the river. She's young. She doesn't deserve to die."

Feelings so intense filled Clayton, and he feared at

any moment, he was going to break down and cry. It was like this woman sitting before him was a different person. Like she didn't remember speaking to them.

"Then you better go save her," she said. "I don't know of any silver. My papa was a sly man, but he never stole any silver I know of."

He glanced up at her caretaker and she shook her head.

"Now tell me what you young men are going to do to save this man's wife," she asked.

Stepping back, Clayton had never felt such despair. Anguish filled him. The woman had lost her mind. Yesterday she seemed fine, and today, she had no memory. Maybe it was all lies and she had nothing to do with the silver or the map.

Seth took him by the arm. "Thank you, Granny Bailey, but we should go."

They walked down the hall to the door and out. Once they were in the yard, Clayton shook his head. "She doesn't remember speaking to us."

Just then the door to the house opened and the servant walked out.

"I'm sorry, gentleman. She had a good day when you spoke to her yesterday. Some days she's fine, and other days, she doesn't know her own name. I remember what she said to you. You're right. I think she has the map. I'll try to press her further later today."

"Thank you," Clayton said.

Harley ran his hand over his face. "That poor woman."

The sheriff shook his head. "Sad. She was fine just the day before."

As they walked back to the sheriff's office, they were silent. Once inside, they all glanced at each other.

"What do we do now?"

The three men flopped down in chairs and stared at one another.

"Anyone got a plan?" Harley asked.

There was no way he was going to let them kill Rena, but how could he stop them, and for that matter, was she still alive even now? Their other victims, they had tortured to death.

"I'd like to tell them that Granny Bailey has the map, but then she doesn't remember anything. That wouldn't be right, but damn, I'm tempted. If they came into town, it would be easier to catch them," Seth said.

"I'll trade myself for her," Clayton said.

"Why would they want you? You're not the map," Harley said. "They want the map."

"Maybe I should break into Granny Bailey's house and find it," Clayton said.

Seth shook his head. "Think about all the knick-knacks and shelves and drawers she has and it could be locked up in a safe somewhere."

"What if we draw a map and make it look authentic by making it look old? Once we have Rena back, then we try to capture them."

There was silence as the three sat contemplating this latest plan. A plan that didn't feel safe by any means, but then even if they had the map, would they just hand over Rena? No, it felt like a setup that they were blindly going into with nothing on their side.

"That's the best idea we've had so far. Can any of you draw?"

"I can," Clayton said, thinking of how he used to draw in school.

"We need some landscape marks that will help make it appear real," Seth said.

"I say we ride out and camp along the Guadalupe tonight. Maybe we could find them in advance. You can add in what you see that would make the map look authentic."

The men began to stir. Seth went to find paper and Clayton a charcoal. Right now, he'd draw a map straight to hell for Jack Bell to follow if he would give him Rena.

Seth cleared his desk, and after several tries, Clayton had drawn the river and some possible land features.

"Let's go," Clayton said. "I can finish this when we get to where we want to camp."

Soon they were riding toward the area of the Guadalupe that the outlaws were to meet them. As Clayton rode, all he could think about was Rena. In the short time they had been together, he realized that if something happened to her, he would be devastated. He wanted a life with this woman. Children and a place to raise them together. With or without Harley. Somehow he'd fallen in love with her and he couldn't live without her.

With an ache in his chest, he rode into battle to save his love.

CHAPTER 21

The next morning as the sun rose, Harley knew what he had to do. It was his fault that Rena was in danger, and he would be the one to get her out.

They had already packed up their camp in order to leave as quickly as possible. Their horses were saddled, and they stood near the hangman's tree on the Guadalupe River, waiting, watching. It was tempting to have his pistol out and shoot the man when he came into view. But he feared for Rena's life.

Clayton had the map rolled up in his hand. It was a fake, but hopefully, it would buy them the time they needed.

The sound of horses had them all turning toward the noise as the two in the Red Jack Gang rode up with

Rena on the back of Jack's horse. Harley did not like seeing her close to that evil man. They pulled to a stop not far from the three lawmen.

"Do you have the map?"

Clayton held it up. "Yes."

"Good, give it to me," Jack said.

"Not until you hand over Rena," Clayton replied.

The man laughed. "No. This is how it's going to work. You give me the map and we'll take Rena and find our treasure. That way we know it's for real."

Harley had expected something like this. "No, this is how it's going to work. We give you the map and you give us Rena. Then I'll go with you to the treasure sight to make certain there is no double cross. Do you understand me?"

The man sat on his horse thinking. "Why do I think there is a double cross coming?"

"Think what you want. We have the map. No Rena, no map," Clayton said.

Harley took the map from Clayton, walked over to where his horse was tethered and gathered the reins.

He held up the map and glared at Jack. "Do you want the map? It's the promise of all your dreams coming true. Take me and the map and give us Rena."

"No," Rena cried.

Jack turned to smack her and Clayton cocked his gun. "I wouldn't if I were you."

He turned back to find all the men's guns pointed on him. But Tray had his gun pointed at Rena.

Smiling, Jack gave a half-hearted grin. "All right."

Rena slid down the side of his horse and all but ran to Harley.

"No, don't do this. They will kill you," she said. "I know. They're planning on killing all of us."

Harley held her tightly against him and rubbed her back as she cried softly against his chest. How had he let his own selfish desires hurt her? If he came back, things would be different.

"Harley, I was so hurt by what you said because I love you. And I don't want you to die. I want you near me. Please, don't do this. Let's make a run for it."

His heart wrenched with pain at her words. No one, not even his father or his mother, had ever told him that they loved him. Sure, he knew he was a bully, a mean person who wore a badge and yet Rena was telling him she loved him with all his flaws. She accepted him and loved him regardless.

"If I don't come back, have a good life with Clayton."

Sobs came from Rena. "No, Harley, don't do this. I'm afraid."

"It will be all right. You've been the best thing that has ever happened to me," he said, his chest constricting. If he was going to die, he had to let her know how happy she made him. He'd been the dick, messing everything up. "I'm sorry. My life would have been very happy with you in it."

"Come on," Jack said. "I'm about to put a bullet in both of you. Enough already. We're going to find that silver today."

Harley set Rena away from him and walked to his horse to lead the man who would soon kill him away from his friends. As long as Rena was safe, he didn't mind dying. She'd shown him what true love could be like. She'd given him a sliver of happiness in his otherwise dark world and for that he would forever be grateful.

Clayton pulled Rena behind him just as Harley reached Jack. "You're a fucking bastard."

"You're damn right I am," he said. "Give me the map."

Just then a wagon came rumbling up to the site with about ten riders who all had their guns out and trained on the pair.

Stunned, Harley saw Granny Bailey sitting in the wagon with a hat on her head.

"Jack," she yelled in her crackly voice, "you looking for this map?"

"You son of a bitch, you were trying to double cross

me," Jack said, spurring his horse toward the old woman.

"You deserved it," Harley yelled after him.

The man rode up to her wagon. "You old witch, you've had it all along."

"Of course, I have. And how many men have you killed trying to find it? Your mother would be so disappointed in you. But then again, you had a worthless father."

Jack's face turned red and his hands were shaking with rage. "Did you find the silver?"

"Honey, that silver has been gone for a long time. Thirty years at least. My son used it to start the mercantile. The rest is safely residing in the bank where you can't get your hands on it."

With a scream, Jack yanked out his gun and before anyone could stop him, he shot Granny Bailey in the chest.

With a slump, she fell over while Seth shot Jack.

"You son of a bitch," Clayton said, running to the old woman.

Her caretaker was cradling her in her arms. Tears running down her face. "Granny?"

"It's all right, Mary Lou, I've been wanting to die for a long time. He just sent me over the edge. I'm going to a far better place than he is." She glanced up at the heavens and sighed as her eyes slowly closed.

Speechless, they all stood staring at the woman who, at almost ninety, had come out to help save Rena's life and brought a bad man to justice.

The men on horseback all removed their hats and bowed their heads.

Harley felt tears well up in his eyes at how the old woman had fought for what was right.

Her caretaker raised her eyes to Clayton and Harley. "Yesterday, she was having such a bad day when you came by. Then, it was like she was her old self and when I told her what happened, she wanted to come and give you the map. She wanted to tell Jack that he was wasting his time, that the silver was gone."

Horse's hooves pounded the ground and they all watched as Tray spurred his horse. Seth grinned.

"Don't worry. We'll catch him."

Rena rushed over to Harley and took him in her arms. "Thank you for trying to save me."

He kissed her on the forehead. "I love you, Rena. I love you and I would have died for you."

CHAPTER 22

Today the town turned out in full to celebrate the life of Granny Bailey. Jack Bell was dead and his partner had been caught dressed like a woman trying to get on a stage out of town. His disguise didn't work when a woman saw through his veil and alerted the stagecoach driver.

Seth had enjoyed slapping the cuffs on him in female clothing. And the men in the jail had all whistled when he came in.

Lillian had gone into labor the night they returned home from the shooting, and ironically, she asked Rena to come assist in the baby's birth.

What a miracle. Seeing their baby girl born had been an honor that Rena felt in awe to witness. Now she couldn't wait for them to have their children.

Hopefully, after everything that happened, Harley would decide to stay. But whatever he chose to do, she would always love him. This had to be his decision.

The three of them walked into the house and sank down on the horsehair couch.

"We need to talk," Rena said. "So much has happened and we haven't had a chance to discuss our marriage."

The men gazed at her like they would rather not, but she knew they needed to clear the air. "I'm sorry that I was so angry at Harley that I didn't tell him where I was going. The two of you had been protecting me and I don't think this would have happened if I had listened and obeyed you."

"True," Clayton said. "And you will be punished for of your lack of obedience. This is why we were guarding you. So that Jack Bell and that Tray would not harm you."

"No, we're not going to punish Rena," Harley said, and Clayton jerked around to stare at him.

"Why not?"

"Because if she hadn't been angry with me, then she would have told me where she was going. If I hadn't been dishonest with her, then none of this would have happened. My own selfish pride was what led to this disaster. And I'm just thankful she wasn't hurt or killed."

Clayton smiled. "Are you still going to Dallas?"

Harley smiled. "Yes. I need to end that chapter of my life. Will I stay? No, because I can't wait to get back here. Rena, you're my wife and I'm pledging to you my heart, my love, and the rest of my days will be spent with you by my side."

She stood and flew into his lap and kissed him. "I don't want you to leave because I'll worry and miss you, but I understand why you have to go. Sometimes, Harley Kerr, you can be a bully, but you're my bully and I love you with all my heart."

"Not a bully, a beast," Clayton said.

"Well, the beast is being tamed by Rena," he said, leaning his head against her chest. "We've told you about our past. But you've said very little about your family."

For a moment, it was quiet before Rena spoke. "My mother was a sickly woman and she died giving birth. My papa was working in the barn and just keeled over one day. When I found him, he was dead. I've been alone for three years. No brothers or sisters, aunts or uncles, not many friends, just alone. Every night, I prayed that a man would come along. Now it seems my prayers have been answered, because I've been saved from my boring existence by not one husband but two. And I thank God for the both of you every day."

Silence filled the room and she curled up in Harley's

lap, so afraid that he would never return to her. "Please come back to me."

"I will," he promised. "But right now, I need to feel my wife's naked arms around me."

"Me too," Clayton said. "It's been a weird couple of days. Time to find happiness with you."

Rena couldn't wait to experience the joy she always found in her husbands' arms. Standing, she took each man by the hand. "Let's go to bed."

They walked into the guest bedroom and began to remove their clothes. Rena stood watching them, the memory of realizing she'd been captured overwhelmed her for a moment. She deserved to be punished for leaving without telling Harley.

"Clayton, sweetie, I need you to spank me tonight."

"You got it. Get undressed and lay on your arms and stick your ass in the air. I can't wait to paddle your ass."

Slowly she began to unbutton her dress. "Just not as hard as Harley," she said.

"No, you do not get to tell me how to spank you," he said as he turned her to the bed.

"You've not said if Jack or Tray harmed you," Harley said, pulling his shirt from his pants. He sat to remove his boots. Then he removed his pants, his big cock jutting out in front of him.

"No, they tried to scare me more than anything. If

you had not come for me, I'm sure I would be dead. But I knew you would come and that frightened me even more."

"We feared they would harm you to get back at us," Clayton said, removing his boots and then his pants.

He walked over to the dresser where he selected a larger plug from the wooden box and a jar of ointment. "This is the last plug. I want to see you work this into your ass. Afterward, I'm going to spank you and you are not allowed to come."

She tilted her blonde curls in one direction. "Yes, I deserve to be punished."

Nothing would have happened if she had told Harley where she was going because he would have insisted on going with her. He would not have allowed her to get into that carriage without checking with the driver and making certain he was one of Lillian's men.

"Never leave without telling one of us," Clayton said. "When we can't find you or don't know where you are, it frightens us. We never want to lose you."

"As long as you do the same for me. I need to know where my men are in case I need them. I'll promise to always let you know if you'll do the same."

The men smiled. "We will," Harley said, answering for them.

"Tonight, once we think you're ready, we're going to

claim you, together. Clayton will take your pussy and me your ass," Harley said, handing her the last plug. "Put it in."

Pursing her lips, she glanced between them and then took the plug. Clayton handed her the lube and watched as she greased up the end. She placed the object between her legs but paused.

"This marriage of ours is different from anything I've ever experienced. Even though I broke the rules, I like the fact that you're in control. I like what we do together. I like it when you spank me, but not when you're angry."

"But you asked me to punish you," Clayton said to her.

She bit her bottom lip. "Yes, because I feel responsible for what happened. If I had spoken to Harley, none of this would have happened."

"Shhh," Harley said. "We all made mistakes. Let's just do better from now on. Let's trust one another, even when we're angry."

Rena smiled at Harley as she reached up and stroked his face.

"Put it in," Harley told her, placing a hand on her knee, she dropped her legs open wide and rubbed the plug through her wet, glistening pussy. The anticipation of both of them claiming her had her pussy throbbing.

Slowly, she inched the plug in, breathing deeply pushing and pulling. She bit her lip as the fake cock popped into place. For a moment, she simply breathed as her body adjusted to the new, larger size. There were no other plugs, this was the end, and tonight she would experience both of her husbands at the same time.

Now they could finally claim her as theirs and she couldn't wait.

"Good girl," Clayton said.

Clayton swatted her ass sending ripples up through the plug sending tingles through her body. She gasped and turned her gaze on him.

"Over my knee," Clayton demanded as he sank down onto the bed.

Harley stood to the side and helped her up and over Clayton's lap before he began to stroke his long, hard cock. Rubbing the bead of come that spilled from the end, Rena watched mesmerized.

Clayton leaned down and kissed her on the ass, running his tongue along the seam of her cheeks. "No one messes with our woman and you're ours. Do you understand?"

"Yes," she whispered. "Make me yours."

This was what she needed. What she wanted. Her two men to show her they cared.

Clayton raised his hand and connected his palm with her rounded cheeks.

Smack!

Harley gripped her breasts in his hands, massaging and twisting her nipples. Explosions of desire were coming from so many places on her body that she moaned.

"Clayton," she cried out, her hands searching for something to grip onto.

Smack, he paddled her again and again in rapid succession.

Another moan escaped.

To change the rhythm, he spanked her first rapidly and then slowly and methodically, taking care to make certain that her entire ass went from white to a blushing pink.

"Clayton," she moaned, feeling so close to coming. Though she knew that Harley had spanked her harder, Clayton's held more meaning. It was a reminder for her to always trust her men. To obey them. That they would take care of her.

Harley slid his fingers over her folds before he plunged them inside her. When he pulled them out, they could see the wetness. "She's dripping."

She turned and gazed at Clayton, tears spilled down her cheeks.

"Do you trust us?"

"Yes," she sobbed.

She tried to rise, but he put a hand on her back as he pulled her into his arms. She threw her arms around him and clung to him.

"I was so scared. So frightened I would never see you again," she sobbed. "I also feared you getting hurt when you did come for me. Never again. Promise me that will never happen again."

Harley reached out and stroked her hair. "Oh, Rena, until I realized we might lose you, I didn't know how much I loved you. You're our wife, our bride, and soon the mother of our children. If something happened to you, it would be devastating."

Clayton held her tightly. "Yes, we love you. With you, I want to create the family I never had."

She raised her head and gazed at them. "I love both of you. You've made my life complete."

Picking her up, Harley laid her on the bed on her back. Immediately, she spread her legs wide.

The time for punishment was over. "Do you still want to come?"

A smile spread across her face. "Yes. I need both of you. I'm ready for you both to claim me. Make me yours."

"Yes, you are," Clayton said. "And we can't wait to fuck you."

Her ass was warm and ached, but beneath the pain was pleasure that rode her hard. Lying on the bed, she was anxious, and her body ached for her men to fill her. Never in a million years had she dreamed that pleasure could come from pain, and she liked that her men took charge of her and were rough and domineering.

Never had she dreamed that two men would satisfy her in ways she never imagined. For days, she'd stretched and trained her ass. Even now, the largest plug resided deep inside her, waiting for her men to remove it. Waiting for them to claim her ass.

While she trembled with anticipation, she couldn't wait to feel them deep inside her at the same time.

Harley rubbed lube over his long hard cock.

Clayton lay beside her and then pulled her on top of him. His big blue eyes gazed into hers. "Are you ready?"

"Yes," she whispered.

On the bed, he lay back, his head on the pillows, his cock standing at attention. All for her, and her pussy clenched as she stared at his massive cock. She could hardly wait to be filled by him.

"Ride me," Clayton said with a groan.

Gladly, she lifted a leg over him and climbed on top, her hands resting on his chest. Leaning on him, she realized the strength of Clayton. All man. Powerful and seductive. Her man.

The bed shifted and Harley climbed behind her. His tongue caressed her cheeks as she hovered over his partner's dick. Licking his way down, he flicked her clit before he sucked it into his mouth. A groan escaped her and she pushed back, needing more of his tongue, but he pushed her toward Clayton's cock.

"I need your pussy gripping me when I bury my cock deep inside you."

And she could hardly wait to have him deep inside her. She repositioned above Clayton and then slid down over his hard cock, piercing her eager, wet pussy. At the feel of him, she leaned back as she went lower and lower until she hit his pelvis. The feel of his long, hard cock snug in her pussy was almost enough to send her over the edge. The plug in her ass was tight against him.

All the pleasure from before returned like a hurricane battering her with greedy lust. She gasped. Filled with cock and the plug, she was so full, so tight, and yet she wanted more.

She wanted Harley.

She began to move up and down on Clayton's rigid member, rubbing her clit, needing to ride the pleasure building inside her.

Harley's hand caressed her buttocks, his hand rubbing her ass, pressing her toward Clayton.

As she hovered over Clayton's chest, her nipples brushed against his hair, rubbing and abrading them. He gripped her face and kissed her. A moan escaped her as their tongues tangled, and still, she wanted more.

She wanted both of her men. Inside her now.

Harley pulled the plug from her ass with one hand while the other one fondled her clit. When the plug came free, she felt like she was opened wide, empty and bereft. A moan escaped her.

"Harley, fuck me."

Leaning over, she felt the flared head of Harley's hard cock press against her trained ass. Slick and hot, the pressure of his invasion grew. Slowly he pushed his rock-hard cock into her, her muscles quivered with submission as he filled her, stretching her.

"Aargh," she cried.

"Relax, honey. It will be easier if you relax," Clayton told her.

With both of them in her body, she felt like there was no room. And yet, her body surrendered, the tight ring of muscle giving way as his cock slid deeply inside her. When he was completely in, he paused letting her adjust to the feel of him. Both of her husbands were now inside her body, and she was completely filled.

"Squeeze me, Rena, squeeze me hard," Harley gasped.

When she clenched her muscles, she felt as if she were attacking and holding hostage both men. Both of their cocks stuffed inside her.

Taking a breath, she moaned as he moved in farther, then retreated, the feel of him hard and thick and so wonderful.

A hot rush of desire raced through her as she accepted him into her body, loving the feel of both men. Pinned between them, she whimpered at how they controlled her completely. They began to move, and she gasped, crying out at the rush of feelings.

First, Clayton, then Harley, each pushing her closer and closer to the edge as they retreated and then filled her over and over. Between them, they maneuvered her body, bringing them all to the brink of pleasure.

Harley pounded into her with Clayton retreating. Between these two men was where she belonged. Here was her life. She needed the two of them to fuck her. To claim her. To make her theirs.

They were her men. Her husbands, her lovers. And she couldn't live without them.

"Please, can I come?" she cried, knowing she couldn't hold out much longer.

"Come all over my cock," Clayton gasped.

"Milk my cock. Take it deep and squeeze it," Harley cried.

With a bright burst of light, a scream tore through her throat as she squeezed and held her men, working the seed from their bodies. They were hers and she was theirs.

Pleasure filled her and their hot seed coated her insides. First, Clayton, and then Harley, as they held her between them, their cocks buried deep inside her.

No barriers remained between them. They had marked her, made her theirs. And joy filled her at the thought of their life together.

All her prayers had been answered. Now she had two husbands and hopefully soon a baby.

Breathing heavily, they reluctantly pulled free from her, but held her between them. Slowly, they returned to normal, but she knew nothing would ever be the same. Her life with her husbands was perfect in every sense of the word.

"I love both of you," she whispered as she lay between them. "You are my heart and my soul. You have rescued me from the lonely life I was living, and I can't wait to see what our future holds."

CHAPTER 23

Twelve months later, Rena looked around the room and smiled. Lillian and her husbands had brought their children over to see the new baby.

"Have you changed a diaper yet," Seth asked Clayton.

"A couple," Clayton said.

Rena laughed as she held their son in her arms. "Only when he has to. Harley is the one who jumps up whenever our son cries."

Harley grinned at her. The trip to Dallas had been good for the man. He'd returned feeling at peace. While he was there, his father passed away in his sleep. It seems the old man knew he had done wrong by Harley and his siblings. And while none of them were close to their father, they forgave him. In the end, he had left all the children twenty thousand dollars and the youngest son he'd left the store to.

When Harley came home, a heavy burden seemed to have lifted from his shoulders and the beast had not returned with him. The bully was no more, and in his place, a gentle man.

He arrived a month before the baby was due, and together, he and Clayton had treated her like a queen.

The sheriff lifted a gunny sack. "We found something among Tray's things that we thought you might like to have back," Will said. He pulled out her father's gold pocket watch.

Tears filled her eyes at the moment. "Oh my, thank you so much, My papa's watch. I thought I would never see it again."

Will handed it to Harley and he brought it to her. Somehow things had come full circle.

"How's Beth?" Rena asked.

"She's walking and getting into everything she finds. You'll soon find out," Lillian said as she glanced at the baby. "May I hold him?"

"Of course," Rena said though a part of her hated to let him go. She felt this urge to keep him near her at all times.

"Oh, look at those tiny fingers. He's so handsome," she said as she cuddled him close.

Suddenly he began to fuss. "It's feeding time."

Lillian reached down and hugged her close. "You are so very blessed to have two wonderful husbands and now a son. We are such lucky women to have not one man, but two, who love us."

Rena smiled. The words were so true. She glanced at her husbands and remembered those first few weeks of marriage. "You are so right, Lillian. I couldn't ask for two better men. And now we have a family."

I LOVE these books because I know at the end I'm going to give my couple a happy ending and a family. Harley quickly became one of my favorite characters and I hoped you enjoyed him as much as I did. He was such a tortured soul and Rena helped him find happiness. I took some liberties with history. Jean Lafitte did sink a large amount of stolen silver on the Sabine River, which was supposedly never found. For my story, I had someone steal that silver and hide it on the Guadalupe river.

What's next? Two Cowboys Save Christmas. Continue reading for a sneak peak.

Christmas Rawls loved helping the children of the orphanage decorate the cedar tree for the holiday. Unless the women in town brought the children presents, there would be nothing under the tree. Such was the life of an orphan.

Outside, the cold wind rattled the windows in the old house, seeping inside. She would need to bundle the little ones tightly tonight to keep them warm in the drafty rooms.

"Jennifer, can you put the paper star on the top?"

The girl reached up and tied it onto the tree, where it promptly fell over.

"Let me do it," David said. The boy moved the hand-cut design farther down the stem, and then with a bow, managed to keep the star on top. At thirteen, he would soon be leaving to find his way on his own.

Christmas stared at each of the children. Each one had arrived in their own special way. Each held a special place in her heart. Christmas hated the idea of having to leave; she loved the children and took care of them. They were her family. They made her happy.

On Christmas day, she would turn twenty. She knew it was time to go, but this was the only home she'd ever known. As a toddler, she'd been left on the doorstep on Christmas Eve, and the lady who ran the orphanage named her Christmas.

Mrs. Griffin had long since died, and now the place was run by Mr. Stephens, who cut corners and tried to make the place profitable, but with twenty mouths ranging in age from two to twenty, it was difficult.

One of the smaller kids, Benjamin, jumped up and down happily. "Santa?"

"That's right, Santa will arrive in one week," she told them.

At her age, she was accustomed to not receiving gifts, but for the sake of the children, she hoped the town would remember them during this special time of year.

The babies were adopted, but the older children usually remained until they left on their own. She was the eldest there; those older had already gone into the world. Some in the middle of the night. Those were the troubling ones. Especially the young women. Where had they gone? Why hadn't they said good-bye?

Mr. Stephens walked out of his office and stared at their makeshift tree. "Time for bed."

Turning, she glanced at the man whose presence she avoided. When he gazed at her, it was like he undressed her with his eyes, and the thought made her shiver with revulsion. There was something about him that had her intuition warning her to stay far away.

"Come children and I'll tuck you in."

As the twelve little ones and eight older children

climbed the groaning stairs under where the roof leaked, she couldn't help but think of this place as home. It was all she knew, and yet if repairs were not soon made, the place would fall down around their ears.

With a shiver, she helped the toddlers change into sleeping clothes. This was her favorite time of night. When she put the little ones to bed, read to the older children, then ushered them into the main room where they all slept.

After everyone was settled in for the night, she undressed and crawled into bed. She turned down the lantern to where she could read from the latest book she borrowed from those donated to the home. Here, she could disappear into a story and not worry about her future.

Mr. Stephens opened the door. "Christmas, I need to see you."

"Yes, sir," she said as she waited for him to close the door before she rose from the bed.

"What do you think he wants?" Jennifer asked her. At fourteen, the girl was often anxious. She worried about everything.

"Oh, probably one of the little ones is sick. You know he doesn't like to care for them when they're ill."

The man didn't seem to like children and it was one

of the reasons she stayed. Who would care for them if she weren't here?

Crawling out of bed, she picked up her wrapper and put it around herself. He had never entered the room this late at night and a trickle of unease wound itself around her middle.

Before she went downstairs, she checked on the toddlers. They were fast asleep. Nervous flutters settled in her stomach as she hurried down the creaking stairs.

When she stepped into his office, two men jumped from behind the door. They were rough looking and hadn't seen a razor or a bath in a long time.

"She'll do," the man said as he shoved a bandana between her lips.

"Told you she was a beauty," Mr. Stephens said.

Fear sparkled down her spine and she struggled to get away, but her hands were being pulled behind her back and tied. The other man placed a tow sack over her head engulfing her in darkness.

"Damn shame to hide all this beauty. But where you're going, it will make you lots of money."

What in the hell was he referring to?

She screamed, but only garbled sounds came from between her lips.

"Here's the cash," she heard the man say.

"Tell the madame she owes me a free sample," Mr. Stephens said.

Dear God, Mr. Stephens was selling her. But to whom? Madame who?

Hands wrapped around her upper arms, and they dragged her from the room and out the door of the house. The cold night air seeped beneath her bed clothes. All she wore was her nightgown, wrapper, and bloomers. She began to fight in earnest, knowing that once they put her in that wagon, she would never return to the orphanage.

"Stop fighting," the man said. "Don't make me hurt you."

Tears trickled down her face. Not even a chance to say good-bye to the children. Who would take care of them?

She felt herself lifted into a wagon and then they were riding away from the only home she had ever known.

Sobs shook her body. What would become of her now? Who had that bastard sold her too?

PLEASE LEAVE A REVIEW

Did you enjoy the book? Reviews help authors. I would appreciate you posting a review.

Follow Lacey Davis on Facebook.

Sign up for my new book alert at https://www.subscribepage.com/laceydavis_author and receive a complimentary book.

Also By Lacey Davis

Blessing, Texas Series
Loving My Cowboys
Two Cowboys' Christmas Bride
Two Cowboys One Bride
Two Cowboys Too Perfect
Two Cowboys to Protect Her
Two Cowboys Save Christmas
Box Set 1
Box Set 2

Bridgewater Brides World
Their Perfect Bride
Their Tempting Bride
Their Scandalous Bride
Box Set

Return to Blessing, Texas
Come Home to the Cowboys
Come Home to the Ranch
Come Home to the Lawmen
Come Home to the Country
Come Home to the Doctor's
Come Home to the Bride

Return to Blessing, Texas Books 1-3
Return to Blessing, Texas Books 4-6

Treasure Falls Brides
Our Fugitive Bride
Our Desperate Bride
Our Wild Bride
Our Dangerous Bride
Our Lucky Bride
Our Christmas Bride
Box Set 1
Box Set 2

Want to learn about my new releases before anyone else? Sign up for my New Book Alert and receive a complimentary book. Blindfold Me.

ABOUT THE AUTHOR

Lacey Davis is a pseudonym for a USA Today bestselling author who wanted to try her hand at writing sexy romance. With these novels, I hope to write sizzling romances that will leave you grabbing a fan to cool yourself off.

If you like hunky bad boy heroes who like to be in charge and strong pretty women who are willing to risk it all, then look no further. These sexy reads will get you in the mood. Come experience strong women who will tame these bad boys and leave them wanting more.

The End

www.ingramcontent.com/pod-product-compliance
Lightning Source LLC
Chambersburg PA
CBHW070003180726
48002CB00019B/1894